Trafalgar

a novel

Angélica Gorodischer

WITHDRAWN

Translated by
Amalia Gladhart

Work published within the framework of "Sur" Translation Support Program of
the Ministry of Foreign Affairs and Culture of the Argentine Republic. Obra ed-
itada en el marco del Programa "Sur" de Apoyo a las Traducciones del Ministerio
de Relaciones Exteriores y Culto de la República Argentina.

Small Beer Press
Easthampton, MA

Small Beer Press
150 Pleasant Street #306
Easthampton, MA 01027
www.smallbeerpress.com
www.weightlessbooks.com
info@smallbeerpress.com

Distributed to the trade by Consortium.

Library of Congress Cataloging-in-Publication Data

Gorodischer, Angélica.
Trafalgar : a novel / Angélica Gorodischer ; translated by Amalia Gladhart. -- 1st ed.
    p. cm.
ISBN 978-1-61873-032-9 (ALK. PAPER) -- ISBN 978-1-61873-033-6 (EBOOK)
I. Gladhart, Amalia. II. Title.
PQ7798.17.073T713 2013
863'.64--DC23

                        2012035130

First edition 1 2 3 4 5 6 7 8 9

Text set in Centaur MT.

Printed on 50# 30% PCR recycled Natures Natural paper by in the USA.

Contents

To
Hugo Gorodischer

Plus loin que le fleuve qui gronde,
Plus loin que les vaste foreês
Plus loin que la gorge profonde,
Je fuirais, je courrais, j'irais'.

Victor Hugo

MEDRANO, TRAFALGAR: Born in Rosario, 2 October, 1936. Only child of Doctor Juan José Medrano Sales, the city's eminent clinician, who was chaired professor of Physiology in the College of Medical Sciences of the Universidad Nacional del Litoral and president of the Medical Society of Rosario, and his wife, Doña Mercedes Lucía Herrera Stone. He received his primary and secondary education at the Marist Brothers' school. His parents hoped he would study medicine, but after a brief incursion into the university cloisters, the young Medrano chose to dedicate himself to commerce, an activity for which he undoubtedly possessed uncommon gifts, and from which he obtained great satisfaction, not solely in financial terms. The tragic deaths of Dr. Medrano Salles and Doña Mercedes Herrera in an automobile accident will be remembered. At that time (1966), Trafalgar Medrano was thirty years old, he had consolidated the commercial contacts established some time before, and his position in the world of business could be classified as brilliant. Outside of the expansion, perhaps unprecedented, of his business activity, his life is without—as he never ceases to remark—notable occurrences. He is single. He lives in the large home that belonged to his parents, in a residential neighborhood to the north of the city of Rosario, a big house, a little antiquated but which he refuses to modify, aside from having it painted every two years, and which during his repeated and sometimes extended absences is left in the care of his faithful servants Don Rogelio Bellevigne and Doña Crisóstoma Ríos de Bellevigne. His offices operate in the building located at 1253 Córdoba Street, attended amiably and efficiently these last twenty years (when they moved from those on the top floor in the 700 block of Mitre) by doña Elvira Suárez de Romegiali and the accountant Servidio Cicchetti. He is a member of the Rosario Pelota Club, the Jockey Club, of The Circle, of the Argentine Academy of Lunfardo. At the death of his parents, he donated Dr. Medrano's scientific library to the Medical Society of Rosario. He possesses, however, a very rich and varied library composed of works of narrative, detective stories, and science fiction, whose volumes in some cases originate in unexpected places. He displays extremely simple tastes: fine cuisine, without excesses; fine wines, even more sparingly; cats, music, black coffee, cigarettes, reading (Balzac, Cervantes, Vian, Le Guin, Lafferty, Villon, Borges, Euripides, Métal Hurlant, Corto Maltés, to cite only a few of his favorites); the company of friends, among whom he names with particular affection Ciro Vázquez Leiva; Dr. Hermenegildo Flynn, physician; Sujer and Angélica Gorodischer; Dr. Nicolás Rubino, attorney; Dr. Simeón Páez, also attorney; Miguel Ángel Sánchez; Roberto Brebbia; Carlos Castro; and distinguished poets such as Jorge Isaías, Mirta Rosenberg, Francisco Gandolfo, et cetera. He owns a number of notable works by the visual artists of Rosario, who also figure among his friends. One can admire in his home pictures by Luis Ouvrard, Gustavo Cochet, Juan Grela, Pedro Giacaglia, Hugo Padeletti, Leónidas Gambartes, Francisco García Carrera, Juan Pablo Renzi, Manuel Musto, Augusto Schiavoni, et cetera, and a very beautiful sculpture by Lucio Fontana, the *Smiling Girl*. He habitually frequents the Burgundy, the well-known establishment that has seen pass through its premises in the 1100 block of Córdoba so many of the city's leading personalities, and he collects gramophone records with recordings of tangos by his favorite orchestras.

> (*Who's Who in Rosario*. Edited by the Subcommittee for Public Relations of the Association of Friends of the City of Rosario. Rosario: La Familia Press, 1977.)

From here on, dear reader, kind reader, even before you begin to read this book, I must ask you a favor: do not go straight to the index to look for the shortest story or the one that has a title that catches your attention. Since you are going to read them, for which I thank you, read them in order. Not because they follow chronologically, though there is something of that, but because that way you and I will understand each other more easily.

Thank you.

A.G.

By the Light of the Chaste Electronic Moon

I was with Trafalgar Medrano yesterday. It's not easy to find him. He's always going here and there with that import-export business of his. But now and then he goes from there to here and he likes to sit down and drink coffee and chat with a friend. I was in the Burgundy and when I saw him come in, I almost didn't recognize him: he had shaved off his mustache.

The Burgundy is one of those bars of which there aren't many left, if there are any at all. None of that Formica or any fluorescent lights or Coca-Cola. Gray carpet—a little worn—real wood tables and real wood chairs, a few mirrors against the wood paneling, small windows, a single door and a façade that says nothing. Thanks to all this, inside there's a lot of silence and anyone can sit down to read the paper or talk with someone else or even do nothing, seated at a table with a cloth, white crockery dishes, and real glass, like civilized people use, and a serious sugar bowl, and without anyone, let alone Marcos, coming to bother them.

I won't tell you where it is because one of these days you might have adolescent sons or, worse, adolescent daughters who will find out, and good-bye peace and quiet. I'll give you just one piece of information: it's downtown, between a shop and a *galería*, and you surely pass by there every day when you go to the bank and you don't even see it.

But Trafalgar came over to me at the table right away. He recognized me, because I still have the appearance—all fine cheviot and Yardley—of a prosperous lawyer, which is exactly what I am. We greeted each other as if we had seen each other a few days before, but I calculated something like six months had passed. I made a sign to Marcos that meant, let's see that double coffee, and I went on with my sherry.

"I haven't seen you in a long time," I said.

"Well, yes," he answered. "Business trips."

Marcos brought him his double coffee and a glass of cold water on a little silver plate. That's what I like about the Burgundy.

"Also, I got into a mess."

"One of these days, you're going to end up in the slammer," I told him, "and don't call me to get you out. I don't deal with that kind of thing."

He tried the coffee and lit a black cigarette. He smokes short ones, unfiltered. He has his little ways, like anyone.

"A mess with a woman," he clarified without looking at me. "I think it was a woman."

"Traf," I said, getting very serious, "I hope you haven't contracted an exquisite inclination for fragile youths with smooth skin and green eyes."

"It was like being with a woman when we were in bed."

"And what did you do with him or with her in bed?" I asked, trying to prod him a bit.

"What do you think one does with a woman in bed? Sing Schumann's *Lieder* as duets?"

"Okay, okay, but tell me: what was there between the legs? A thing that stuck out or a hole?

"A hole. Better put, two, each one in the place where it belonged."

"And you took advantage of both."

"Well, no."

"It was a woman," I concluded.

"Hmmm," he said. "That's what I thought."

And he went back to his black coffee and unfiltered cigarette. Trafalgar won't be hurried. If you meet him sometime, at the Burgundy or the Jockey Club or anywhere else, and he starts to tell you what happened to him on one of his trips, by God and the whole heavenly host, don't rush him; you'll see he has to stretch things out in his own lazy and ironic fashion. So I ordered another sherry and a few savories and Marcos came over and made some remark about the weather and Trafalgar concluded that changes of weather are like kids, if you give them the time of day, it's all over. Marcos agreed and went back to the bar.

"It was on Veroboar," he went on. "It was the second time I'd gone there, but the first time I don't count because I was there just in passing and I didn't even have time to get out. It's on the edge of the galaxy."

I have never known if it is true or not that Trafalgar travels to the stars but I have no reason not to believe him. Stranger things happen. What I do know is that he is fabulously rich. And that it doesn't seem to matter a bit to him.

"I had been selling reading material in the Seskundrea system, seven clean, shiny little worlds on which visual reading is a luxury. A luxury I introduced, by the way. Texts were listened to or read by touch there. The rabble still does that, but I have sold books and magazines to everyone who thinks they're somebody. I had to land on Veroboar, which isn't very far away, to have a single induction screen checked, and I took the opportunity to sell the surplus." He lit another cigarette. "They were comic books. Don't make that face—if it hadn't been for the comic books, I wouldn't have had to shave my mustache."

Marcos brought him another double coffee before he could order it. That Marcos is a marvel: if you drink nothing but dry sherry, well chilled, like me; or orange juice—not strained—with gin, like Salustiano, the youngest of the Carreras; or seven double coffees in a row like Trafalgar Medrano, you can be sure that Marcos will be there to remember it even if it's been ten years since you went to the Burgundy.

"This time I didn't go to Seskundrea, it wouldn't do for the luxury to become a custom and then I'd have to think up something else, but I was taking aspirin to Belanius III, where aspirin has hallucinogenic effects. Must be a matter of climate or metabolism."

"I'm telling you, you'll end up in the slammer."

"Unlikely. I convinced the police chief on Belanius III to try Excedrin. Imagine that!"

I tried, but I was unable to do so. The police chief of Belanius III abusing himself with Excedrin lies beyond the limits of my modest imagination. And then again, I didn't make a great effort, because I was intrigued by the bit about the woman who probably wasn't one and by the thing about the mess.

"Belanius III is not that close to Veroboar, but once I was there I decided to try with more magazines and a few books, just a few so as not to frighten them. Of course, now I was going to stay a while and I wasn't going to offer them to the first monkey who might appear so he might sell them and keep my cut, forget it. I parked the clunker, put my clothes and the merchandise in a suitcase, and took a bus headed for Verov, the capital."

"And customs?"

He looked at me condescendingly: "On civilized worlds there aren't customs, old man. They're cleverer than we are."

He finished the second coffee and looked toward the bar but Marcos was waiting on another table.

"I was determined to talk to someone strategically situated who could tell me where and how to organize the sale. For a commission."

"So, on civilized worlds there aren't customs, but there are bribes."

"Bah, more or less civilized. Don't be so picky: everyone has their weaknesses. There, for example, I had a big surprise: Veroboar is an aristomatriarchy."

"A what?"

"Just that. A thousand women—I assume they're women; young—I assume they're young; gorgeous."

"You assume they're gorgeous."

"They are. That you can see from a mile away. Rich. You can see that from a mile away, too. They alone hold in one fist all of Veroboar. And what a fist. You can't even sneeze without their permission. I'd been in the hotel two minutes when I received a note on letterhead with seals in which I was summoned to the Governor's office. At 31 hours, 75 minutes on the dot. Which means I had half an hour to bathe, shave, and dress."

Marcos arrived with the third double coffee.

"And unfortunately," said Trafalgar, "save in the homes of The Thousand, although I did not have time to see them, on Veroboar there are no sophisticated grooming devices like those on Sechus or on Vexvise or on Forendo Lhda. Did I ever tell you that on Drenekuta V they travel in oxcarts but they have high-relief television and these cubicles of compressed air that shave you, give you a peel, massage you, make you up—because on Drenekuta men use makeup and curl their hair and paint their nails—and dress you in seven seconds?"

"No, I don't think so. One day you told me about some mute guys that danced instead of talking or something like that."

"Please. Anandaha-A. What a lousy world. I could never sell them anything."

"And did you arrive in time?"

"Where?"

He drank half the cup of coffee.

"At the Governor's office, where else?"

"A magnificent Governor. Blonde, green eyes, very tall, with a pair of legs that if you saw them, you'd have an attack."

He's telling *me* about splendid women. I married one thirty-seven years ago. I don't know if Trafalgar Medrano is married or not. I will only add that my wife's name is Leticia and go on.

"And two hard little apples that you could see through her blouse and some round hips." He paused. "She was a viper. She wasted no spit on ceremony. She planted herself in front of me and said: 'We wondered when you would return to Veroboar, Mr. Medrano.' I thought we had begun well, and I was wrong like an asshole. I told her it was very flattering that they should remember me and she looked at me as if I were a piece of cow manure the street sweeper had forgotten to pick up, and she let fly—do you know what she said to me?"

"No idea."

"'We have not looked favorably upon your clandestine activities in the port of Verov.' What do you say to that?"

I didn't say anything.

"There's no need to recite the whole conversation. Besides, I don't remember it. Those witches had executed the poor guy who tried to sell my comic books," he drank a little more coffee, "and they had confiscated the material and decided I was a delinquent."

"And you took her to bed and convinced her not to execute you, too."

"I did not take her to bed," he explained very patiently.

"But you told me."

"Not that one. After informing me that I had to address her by her title, which was Enlightened Lady in Charge of the Government of Verovsian."

"Don't tell me every time you spoke to her you had to say all that."

"That's what I'm telling you. After informing me, she told me I could not leave the hotel without authorization and that of course I must not try to sell anything and that they would advise me when I could return. If I ever could. And that the next day I had to present myself before the members of the Central Government. And that I should retire."

"Wow."

"I went to the hotel and smoked three packs of cigarettes. I wasn't liking this at all. I had my food brought to my room. The hotel's food was disgusting, and this was the best in Verov, and to top it off the bed was too soft and the window didn't close well."

The remaining coffee was surely cold but he drank it anyway. Marcos was reading the racing section in the paper: he knows everything there is to know about horses and a bit more. He has a son who's a brand-new colleague of mine, and a married daughter who lives in Córdoba. There were no more than two other occupied tables, so the Burgundy was much more peaceful than Veroboar. Trafalgar smoked for a while without speaking and I looked at my empty glass, wondering whether this was a special occasion: I only drink more than two on special occasions.

"The next day I received another note, on letterhead but without seals, in which I was told that the interview was with the Enlightened and Chaste Lady Guinevera Lapis Lazuli."

"What did you say?" I jumped in. "That was her name?"

"No, of course not."

Marcos had put down the paper—he had collected at one of the other tables—and now he was coming with the fourth double coffee. He didn't bring me anything, because this didn't look like a special occasion.

"Her name," said Trafalgar, who never puts sugar in his coffee, "was something that sounded like that. In any case, what they told me was that the interview had been postponed until the next day because the enlightened, chaste and so forth, who was a member of the Central Government, had begun her annual proceedings before the Division of Integral Relations of the Secretariat of Private Communication. The year there lasts almost twice as long as here and the days are longer and so are the hours."

Frankly, I didn't give a damn about Veroboar's chronosophy.

"And what does all that mean?" I asked.

"What did I know?"

He fell quiet, watching three guys who came in and sat down at a table at the back. I'm not sure, but it seems to me one of them was Basilio Bender, the one who has a construction firm, you must know him.

"I found out later, bit by bit," Trafalgar said with the cup of coffee in his hand, "and I don't know if I understood it completely. So the next day, same story, because the enlightened one continued with her proceedings and the next day too and the next day the same. On the fifth day, I tired of the blonde matriarchs and their secretaries, and of being shut up in the hotel room, of the garbage I had to eat and of pacing twenty square meters thinking that likely they would hold me on Veroboar for an indefinite period. Or they'd shoot me."

He broke off for a moment, irritated in retrospect, while he drank the coffee, and that made four.

"Then I bribed the waiter who brought me my food. It wasn't difficult and I had already suspected as much because he was a skinny guy with a hungry face, rotten teeth, and threadbare clothes. Everything is wretched and sad on Veroboar. Everything except for The Thousand. I'll never go back to that lousy world." He thought about it. "That is, I don't know."

I was getting impatient: "You bribed him. And?"

"That scared the guy half to death but he found me a telephone book and he informed me that to interview a member of the Central Government you had to be formally dressed, damn it."

"Traf, I don't understand anything," I practically shouted. "Marcos, another sherry."

Marcos looked at me with surprise, but he took out the bottle.

"Ah, I didn't tell you that in the last of those notes they informed me that since the enlightened one had finished her proceedings, she would remain shut up at home for five to ten days. And since they weren't summoning me to the office, I wanted her home address so as to go see her there."

"But they had forbidden you to leave the hotel."

"Uh-huh."

Marcos arrived with the sherry: a special occasion.

"I had to do something. Five to ten days more was too much. So that night, since I didn't know what constituted formal dress on Veroboar and the skinny waiter didn't either—how would he know?— I dressed as if I were going to be a groomsman: tailcoat, white shirt with pearl buttons, satin bowtie, patent leather shoes, top hat, and cape. And walking stick and gloves."

"Go on."

"You can't imagine the things I carry in my luggage. Remind me to tell you what formalwear on Foulikdan is. And what you have to put on if you want to sell anything on Mesdabaulli IV," he laughed; I won't say hard, because Trafalgar isn't very expressive, but he laughed. "Once dressed, I waited for the signal from the skinny guy and when he informed me over the house phone that there was no one downstairs, I left the hotel and took a taxi that was already waiting for me and that covered some five kilometers at a man's pace. We arrived. My God, what a house. Of course, you don't know what houses are like on Veroboar. Scarcely better than a slum. But Guinevera Lapis Lazuli was one of The Thousand and a member of the Central Government. Old man, what a palace. Everything in marble and crystal half a meter thick in a garden filled with flowers and fountains and statues. The night was dark. Veroboar has a rickety little moon that gives almost no light, but there were yellow lamps among the plants in the garden. I crossed it, walking briskly as if I lived there, and the taxi driver watched me open-mouthed. I reached the door and looked for a bell or a knocker. There was none. Nor was there a door handle, but if there was anything I couldn't do, it was stand there waiting for a miracle. I pushed the door and it opened."

"You went in?"

"Of course I went in. I was sure they were going to shoot me. If not that night, the next day. But I went in."

"And?"

"They didn't shoot me."

"I had already noticed that."

"There was no one inside. I coughed, clapped my hands, called. No one. I started walking randomly. The floors were marble. There were huge, round lamps hanging from the ceiling on chains encrusted with stones. The furniture was of gilded wood, very elaborately worked."

"What do I care about the decoration of Lapis Lazuli's house? Do me the favor of telling me what happened."

As you see, I preach but I don't practice. Sometimes Trafalgar drives me nuts.

"For a while, nothing happened. Until somewhere around there I pushed on a door and I found her."

The sherry was good and cold, and the guy I think was Bender got up and went to the bathroom.

"Was she blonde, too?" I asked.

"Yes. You'll excuse me, but I have to talk about the decoration of that room."

"If there's no other choice."

"There isn't. It was monstrous. Marble everywhere in various shades of pink on the walls and the floor, and black on the ceiling. Artificial plants and flowers sprouted from the baseboards. Plastic. In every color. Corner cupboards holding censers with incense. Above shone a fluorescent moon like a tortilla hung by transparent threads that swayed when I opened the door. Next to one wall there was a machine the size of a sideboard that buzzed and had little lights that turned on and off. And against another wall, an endless, golden bed, and she was on the bed, naked and watching me."

I seriously considered drinking a fourth sherry.

"I had prepared a magnificent poem that consisted in not versifying, or in versifying as little as possible, but the scene left me breathless. I took off the top hat, I made a bow, I opened my mouth, and nothing came out. I tried again and I started to stammer. She kept looking at me and when I was about to set in with the whole Enlightened and Chaste Lady, et cetera, she raised a hand and made signs for me to come closer."

I never noticed when, but he had finished the fourth coffee because Marcos arrived with another cup.

"I went closer, of course. I stopped at the side of the bed, and the machine that buzzed was on my right. I was nervous—do the math—and I reached out a hand and started to feel around to see if I could turn it off without taking my eyes off her. It was worth it."

"She was just a woman. What's the big deal?"

"I told you, I think she was. What I'm sure of is that she was really hot. By that point, I was too. With my right hand I found a lever and I lowered it and the machine shut off. Without the buzzing, I started to feel better. I bent down and I kissed her on the mouth, which evidently was the right thing under the circumstances because she grabbed me by the neck and started to pull downward. I tossed the top hat away and used my two free hands for the two little apples, this time without a blouse or anything."

"Nice night."

"More or less, you'll see. I undressed in record time, I threw myself on top of her and I said something like girl, you're the prettiest thing I've seen in my life, and I assure you I wasn't lying, because she was pretty and warm and I already felt like a gaucho bard and king of the world all in one, and you know what she said to me?"

"How am I going to know? What did she say?"

"She said, 'Mandrake, my love, don't call me girl, call me Narda.'"

10

"Traf, cut the crap."

"It's not crap. I, who was in no state to be thinking in subtleties, charged in with everything, although I felt like I was screwing a nutcase."

"Was she chaste?"

"What do you think? Maybe she was enlightened, but chaste she was not. She knew them all. And between the little screams and the pirouettes, she kept calling me Mandrake."

"And you called her Narda."

"What did I care? She was pretty, believe me, and she was tireless and tempting. Whenever I eased up a bit and dozed, holding her, she ran her fingers and her tongue over me and she laughed at me, poking her nose into my throat, and she nibbled at me and I got back to work and, knotted together, we rolled across the golden bed. Until at some point in one of those somersaults, she wised up to the fact that the machine was shut off. She sat up on the bed and gave a howl and I thought, why such a fuss? It's as if you start howling because the water heater shut down."

"But that wasn't a water heater, I'm just saying, right?"

"No, it wasn't. I wanted to go on with the party and I tried to grab her so she would lie back down but she yelled louder and shouted questions at me, what was I doing there? I said to her, what a terrible memory you have, my dear, and she kept on yelling who was I and what was I doing in her room and I should leave immediately and she tried to cover herself with something."

"Nutcase barely says it," I commented.

"Ah, that's what I thought, but it turned out that no, the poor thing was partly right."

He was quiet for a while and then he remembered I was there. "Did I tell you I had undressed in record time? Well, I dressed even more quickly, I don't know how, because although I didn't understand what was happening, I had the impression that the matter was becoming uglier than I had supposed. And while I grabbed my shirt and held up my pants and stuffed the bowtie into my pocket all at the same time, I thought it would really have been handy to be Mandrake, so as to, with that magnetic sweep of my hand, appear fully dressed. And right then, I knew I was Mandrake."

"But, really!"

"Don't you get it?" he said, a little put out, as if anyone could get anything in all that jumble. "I was dressed like Mandrake and I have, I had, a mustache and black hair, a little slicked down. And The Thousand had confiscated the comic books."

"And Lapis Lazuli had read them and she had fallen in love with Mandrake, I understand that. But why was she yelling if she thought you were Mandrake?"

"Wait, wait."

"Because what more did she want, given the way your little evening was going?"

"Wait, I'm telling you, a person can't tell you anything."

The ashtray was full of unfiltered cigarette butts. I gave up smoking eighteen years ago, and at that moment, I regretted it.

"I finished getting dressed and ran out of there with the cape and the top hat in my hand and without the walking stick or the gloves while the blonde wrapped up in a silk sheet—a golden silk sheet, believe it or not—and threatened me with torture and death by dismemberment. I don't know how I didn't get lost in all that marble. Her screams could be heard all the way to the front door. On the street, not a single taxi. I ran two or three blocks, in the dark, through a silent neighborhood in which surely five or six of The Thousand lived, because each house occupied at least a block. After an avenue wider than that one in Buenos Aires, when the slum began, I found a taxi. The driver was a sallow old man who wanted to talk. Not I. Maybe I would have become sallow, I'm not saying no, but I didn't want to chat. I climbed the stairs three at a time—there was no elevator in that filthy hotel—I went into the room, I took off the tailcoat, I shaved off my mustache, I put on a blond wig—I already told you that on my trips, my luggage has everything—and glasses and a cap and a checked jacket and brown pants and I started putting things into my suitcase. And right in the midst of that the skinny guy, who had taken a special interest in my affairs not thanks to my overpowering personality, but thanks to the possibilities of my billfold, showed up and found me flinging around underwear."

"Tell me, Traf, why were you running away from a handful of women who were stunning and also layable from what I can see, or from what I hear?"

He was midway through the sixth coffee and we were alone in the Burgundy. It was getting late but I didn't even look at the clock, because I didn't plan on leaving until I had heard the end. Leticia knows that occasionally, occasionally, I get home very late, and she doesn't mind, so long as it remains only occasionally.

"You were never on Veroboar," Trafalgar said, "nor did the Governor holler at you, nor did you meet the hungry, fearful skinny guy or the guy they shot for two dozen comic books, an asthmatic mechanic who had purulent conjunctivitis and was missing two fingers on his left hand and wanted to earn a few extra bucks so as to go two days without working at the port. Nor did you see Lapis Lazuli's house. Misery, grime, and mud and stench of sickness and rot everywhere. That's Veroboar. That and a thousand frighteningly rich and powerful women who do whatever they want with everybody else."

"You can't trust women," I said.

I have four daughters: if one of them heard me, she'd strangle me. Especially the third one, who is also a lawyer, God help us. But Trafalgar cut me off at the pass: "From a few things I've seen, you can't trust men, either."

I had to agree and I haven't traveled as much as Trafalgar Medrano. Mexico, the United States, Europe and that, and summers in Punta del Este. But I've never been on Seskundrea or on Anandaha-A.

"It may seem to you that I was, shall we say, too cautious, but you will see I was right. I realized that if the blonde from the Central Government caught me, she'd dismember me for sure."

He finished the coffee and opened another packet of unfiltered black cigarettes.

"The skinny guy gave me a few details when I told him I was in a mess, although I didn't clarify what kind of mess. The position of The Thousand is not hereditary, they aren't daughters of notable families.

They come from the people. Any girl who's pretty, but really pretty, and manages (which is no easy feat or even close) to pull together a certain sum before she starts to get wrinkly, can aspire to be one of The Thousand. If she manages, she repudiates family, past, and class. The others educate her, they polish her, and afterward they set her loose. And the only thing she has to do from there on out is enjoy herself, become richer all the time, because everyone works for her, and govern Veroboar. They don't have sons. Or daughters. They're supposed to be virgins and immortals. People suspect, nevertheless, that they are not immortal. I know they're not virgins."

"Yours wasn't."

"Nor the others, I'd bet my life. They don't have children, but they do make love."

"With who? With The Thousand Males?"

"There are no Thousand Males. I suppose, in secret, among themselves. But officially, once a year, all planned in the Secretariat of Private Communication. They make an application and while they wait for an answer, the rest congratulate them and send them little gifts and have parties. At the Secretariat they always tell them yes, of course, and then they go to their houses, dismiss the servants, set the stage, connect the machine, and lie down. With the machine. The one I turned off. The machine gives them two things: one, hallucinations—visual, tactile, auditory, and everything—which follow the model they've selected and which is already programmed into the apparatus. The model may exist or not, it can be the doorman of the ministry or a creature imagined by them or, in my case, a character from a story in one of the damned comic books that I myself sold to the mechanic. And two, all of the sensations of orgasm. That's why Lapis Lazuli was in seventh heaven with what she believed were the effects of the machine and she thought, I imagine, that the illusion of going to bed with Mandrake was perfect. How could it not be perfect, poor girl, since I had arrived just in time. The electronic romance lasts a few days, the skinny guy didn't know how many, and afterward they return, smug as can be, to govern and to live like kings. Like queens."

"The skinny guy told you all that?"

"Yes. Not as I'm telling you but instead full of mythological flourishes and fabulous explanations. While I put my things in the suitcase. He even helped me. I closed it and ran out because I knew the potatoes were about to burn and I knew why, and the skinny guy ran after me. So much courage had already caught my attention. But while we descended the three floors he started telling me, gasping, that he had a daughter prettier and blonder than Ver."

"Ver?"

"The sun. And that he was saving so that one day she could become one of The Thousand. I stopped short on the second floor and I told him he was crazy, that if he loved her he should marry her to the fried-cakes seller or the cobbler and sit down to wait for her to give him grandchildren. But he was crazy and he didn't hear me, and if he did hear me, he didn't pay any attention: he asked if I was rich. Like I tell you, you can't trust men, either."

"You gave him the money."

"I kept on going down the stairs by leaps and the skinny guy found me a taxi."

"You gave him the money."

"Let's not talk about the matter. I got into the taxi and I told the driver, who I don't know if he was old or if he was sallow or if he was both things or neither, that I would pay him double if he would take me to the port at top speed. He flew and I paid him double. I was looking behind the whole time to see if Lapis Lazuli had set the dogs on me."

"She hadn't set anything on you."

"Are you kidding? I beat them by a hair. I turned on the motors but I was still touching the ground when they arrived with sirens and searchlights and machine guns. They started to shoot and that's when I lifted off. They must have shot all of them for letting me escape. Or maybe they dismembered them in my place."

"What an escape."

He drank his coffee and grabbed his billfold.

"Leave it," I said, "my treat. To celebrate your return."

"I was in no shape to celebrate," he hesitated before putting his billfold away. "I detoured a little and went to Naijale II. You can sell anything there. And buy for a song a plant from which the chemists of Oen derive a perfume that cannot be compared to any other from any other place. Imagine the state I was in that I didn't unload the merchandise and I didn't buy anything. I went to a hotel like a decent person and I spent a week eating well and sleeping as well as I could. Apart from that, the only thing I did was go to the beach and watch television. I did not drink alcohol, I did not look at women, and I did not read comic books. And I assure you that on Naijale II all three are of the first quality. Afterwards, I came home. I had an awful journey, sleeping jumpily, mistaking my route every moment, making calculations that probably aren't worth anything because I don't know how long a pregnancy lasts on Veroboar. I didn't ask the skinny guy and if I had asked him he would have told me about the pregnancy of his wife, who must be an old lady, more scrawny than he, and how do I know if The Thousand have the same physiology as the common women? How do I know they aren't altered? How do I know if they can or can't get pregnant? And if they can, how do I know if Lapis Lazuli got pregnant that night? By Mandrake? How do I know if The Thousand aren't machines too and if they haven't executed (or worse) the skinny guy's daughter just like all those who aspired to be like them, a matter of keeping the money while they keep on making love with other machines?"

"You were in bed with her, Traf. Was she a woman?"

"Yes. I think so."

"Too bad," I said. "If they were machines, you would have no reason to return to Veroboar."

I paid, we stood up, and we left. When we went out, it had stopped raining.

16

The Sense
of the Circle

Encore n'y a il chemin
qui n 'aye son issuë.
Montaigne

Have you seen those houses on Oroño Boulevard, especially the ones that face east, those dry, cold, serious, heavy houses, with grilles but without gardens, maybe at the most a tile patio paved like the sidewalk? In one of those houses lives Ciro Vázquez Leiva, Cirito. Great guy, a little weary, tolerably rich, married to a tiresome and exasperating woman, Fina Ereñú. Every time Fina goes to Salta to visit their daughter and the grandchildren, and fortunately she goes often enough that he does not fall completely silent, Cirito stops going to the Jockey Club and that is when a few friends of the kind who correctly interpret the signs go to the cold, dry house and play poker in the dining room. Exclusively masculine, even somewhat solemn gatherings at which they drink whiskey in moderation and a coffee or two, or liters of coffee if Trafalgar Medrano is there, like last Thursday.

Not that I have ever been there, because as I mentioned, women are just in the way, but Ciro often shows up at Raúl's with the Albino Gamen, who was there. Cirito has incredible luck. At least that's what his friends say who don't want to recognize the truth that, obliged by circumstances, he has developed an infinite sense of opportunity and an infinite ability to distort the truth as necessary, just exactly as much as necessary. And that night, although they play with the same moderation with which they drink whiskey, he won piles of money. Most of all at the expense of the Albino and of Doctor Flynn—the physician, not the lawyer. Trafalgar Medrano, who is more circumspect, came out even. After a catastrophic rematch, the Albino said enough and Flynn said you're an animal, Cirito, and Trafalgar Medrano said, is there no more coffee? There was. The others served themselves whiskey and Cirito put away the cards. The Albino said that the next day he was going to bring a new deck and someone suggested it should be a Spanish one, let's see if playing *truco* Cirito kept sweeping everything before him.

"Bring whatever deck you want," said Cirito, who was happy, "Spanish or Chinese or whatever else."

"Playing cards are Chinese," said the Albino.

"Could be," said Flynn, who is cultured, "but it was the Arabs who brought them to the West. Viterbo says that at the end of the fourteenth century, the Arabs carried them to Spain and that they were called *naib.*"

"And who is that Viterbo?" asked the Albino.

"And that," Flynn continued, "the coins are the bourgeoisie, the cups are the clergy, the swords are the army, and the clubs are the people."

"As always and everywhere," said Cirito.

"I met some guys who were all of that and nothing at the same time," said Trafalgar.

"I know," said the Albino, "and then who made the revolutions, huh?"

"There were none," said Trafalgar. "Not revolutions, not anything."

"Tell," said Cirito.

A rhetorical request, because when Trafalgar begins to tell something like that very slowly, almost in spite of himself, no one can stop him.

"Were any of you ever on Anandaha-A?"

No one, ever, as was to be expected. It isn't easy to go to the places where he goes.

"It's horrible," he said. "The most horrible world you can imagine. When it's day, it seems like it's night, and when it's night, you turn on the strongest light you have and you can barely see your hands because the darkness swallows everything. There are no trees, there are no plants, there are no animals, there are no cities, there is nothing. The land is rolling, with stunted little mountains. The air is sticky; there are a few narrow, lazy rivers and the few people that live there, and at first glance one wonders if they can be called people, take some gray leaves or some worms, I don't know, from the bottom of the rivers, they squash them between their fingers, they mix them with water, and they eat them. Disgusting. The ground is cold and damp, like tamped earth. There is never wind, it never rains, it is never cold, it is never hot. A purplish sun the color of wine sediment always makes the same circuit in the same dirty sky without it mattering to anyone and there are no moons."

"You must have had a lot of fun," said the Albino Gamen.

"Quite a bit," Trafalgar admitted. "A few years ago, I had earned a truckload of dough selling little light bulbs on Prattolva, where they have just discovered electricity, and as I knew something about the useless sun of Anandaha-A, it occurred to me that I might earn another truckload selling them lamps, lanterns, those things that would eat the darkness. But of course what I did not know was that those people had no intention of buying anything, anything at all. I went to Prattolva with another load and on the way back I set down on Anandaha-A close to what seemed to be a small city and which was not a city, small or large, but rather an encampment, but something is something. The welcome could not have been more effusive: the people in the camp had become as bored as penguins and I was a big novelty. I don't know why people choose to study such disagreeable things. Unless it's the usual: the hope of earning something, an attitude to which I adhere and which I consider quite laudable. And that is how there were twelve or fifteen people in the camp, all with ostentatious titles, but they luckily also took the trouble to cook, fix a faucet, play the harmonica or tell dirty stories. And friendly and courteous, all of them. There was that Swedish geologist, Lundgren, who was quite disappointed when he learned I didn't play chess but whose disappointment lifted when I told him I was going to teach him the three varieties of sintu—the combative, the contemplative, and the fraternal—which are played in the Ldora system, one on each of the three worlds. Next to that, chess looks like tic-tac-toe. And I taught him all three and he beat me in just one match, a combative one. I prefer fraternal. There was Doctor Simónides, a little bald Greek who did everything, even psychoanalysis, and who enjoyed everything. There was a chemist, I don't really know what for, Doctor Carlos Fineschi, specialist in river waters, you tell me. An engineer, Pablo María Dalmas. An anthropologist, Marina Solim. A sociologist, an astrophysicist, mechanical engineers, all that. The League of Nations, enough to try to convince God the Father that we're good and we love one another. And there was Veri Halabi, I don't know what her nationality was but what a beauty, please. Almost as pretty as the matriarchs of Veroboar, but with black hair. Expert in comparative linguistics—there is no justice. After five minutes one realized they were all infatuated with her and Fineschi most of all because, as for Marina Solim, she is efficient and maternal and incredibly nice, but she in no way has a figure to inspire erotic daydreams. But between the fact that Halabi was gorgeous but she didn't make you say it and that Doctor Simónides could take someone aside and convince them of just about anything, people got along well and were relaxed. And if they had begun to get bored, it was because they had finished what they had to do, or what remained could be done back here in the university offices and on the kitchen table at home. Save for Veri Halabi, who kept discovering things but who didn't know what they meant, poor girl."

And Trafalgar plugged in the electric coffeepot again and waited. He's like that: when he told Páez about the affair with the machines for making love, he practically drove him crazy, and Fatty Páez is really pretty unflappable. Afterwards he returned to the table and he drank his coffee and the others didn't make a sound, waiting for the next chapter.

"The first day, they just wanted to get the idea of selling anything out of my head. I didn't pay any attention, because the doctors know a lot about science, I'm not saying they don't, but about buying and selling, nothing, old man, nothing. Marina Solim grabbed me and told me the inhabitants of Anandaha-A were practically an extinct species—unfortunately, according to her—although frankly it was hard to understand what she saw in them but as far as that goes, it was also hard to understand what happened afterward. Marina told me theirs was a primitivism bordering on the bestial. They did not build tools, they lived out in the open, they had forgotten about fire if they ever knew how to light a fire, they didn't even speak. They dressed, men and women alike, in these shabby sacks open at the sides that they took, that's what Marina believed, from the dead, because as for weaving, they didn't weave them. They ate, slept wherever, did their business and even copulated in sight of everyone, there were almost no children or pregnant women, and they spent the days lying down without doing anything. And they danced."

Flynn was surprised about the dancing, and the Albino says he tried to give a lecture on the dance as a refined expression, that's just what he said, refined, of a system of civilization, et cetera, but Trafalgar didn't let him say much.

"If you want," he told him, "I'll give you the address and phone number for Marina Solim. She's Chilean but she lives in Paris and she works at the Museum of Man. You go and ask her and you're going to fall flat on your back at what she tells you."

"The only thing I'm saying is . . . ," Flynn began.

"They were like animals, I saw them," Trafalgar said. "Those in the camp, which wasn't called a camp but rather an Interdisciplinary Evaluation Unit, said they were ugly, but to me they seemed very beautiful. Of course, I have seen many more things than those good doctors and lady docs and I know what is ugly and what is pretty. There is almost nothing that is ugly, on that Marina and I are in agreement. Very tall and very thin, with white skin and black hair, long, narrow faces and very big, very open eyes. Toad eyes, said Veri Halabi, who hated them. The others didn't hate them; worse, they were indifferent, save for Marina Solim. At the beginning, Doctor Simónides told me, they had tried to speak with them, but it was as if they neither saw nor heard them. Afterward they had realized that they had either never had or had lost the capacity to communicate and they began to treat them like little animals: they took them food and they clicked their tongues and snapped their fingers at them. But the other guys, nothing: didn't look, didn't sniff, didn't turn their heads when they approached, didn't eat and that even though Dalmas made some crazy good fish stews. Then they decreed they were animals and washed their hands of them. Even Marina Solim was a little disheartened, because the only thing she could do was sit down close to them and pass the hours watching what they did, which was nothing. Live, that's all, if to live is to breathe and eat and shit and copulate and sleep."

"And dance," said Flynn.

"And dance. Until one time Lundgren and Dalmas, who sometimes worked together, found something. Do you know what they found? A book, that's what they found."

"I know," said the Albino, "the *Memoirs of a Russian Princess.*"

"What an imagination you have, man. No. Something very different, although of course it wasn't a book, either."

"So what was it?" said Flynn, who I already told you is cultured but who is also impatient.

"Something like a book. Some very thin leaves, almost transparent, of a metal that looked like shiny aluminum, perforated on one of the longer sides, the left, and bound there with rings of the same material but thick, filiform and soldered no one knew how, or possibly cut from a single piece. And covered with something that anyone could see was writing. They found it while digging at the foot of a hill. They turned things over all around looking for something more but there was nothing. And then it occurred to Lundgren, and he does have imagination because otherwise he would not have been able to learn the three versions of sintu and even beat me in a combative match, the big cretin—and I still wonder how he did it because in sintu there are no coincidences—to dig directly into the hill. All of them practically died: they weren't hills, they were ruins. Covered for thousands and thousands of years by the hard mud of Anandaha-A. Busy taking things out, they didn't even have time to celebrate. Every hill was a house or, better put, a complex of various houses that were connected. There were not only utensils but equipment, machines, furniture, more books, dishes, vehicles, decorations. Everything quite past its prime but recognizable although not identifiable. They really went to town, especially Marina Solim and that precious Halabi. Dalmas and the mechanical engineers racked their brains studying the machines and the artifacts but they couldn't make sense of anything. They classified everything and they prepared it all to be brought back and Marina began to reconstruct, as she said, a prodigious civilization and the only one who was still stymied was Veri Halabi who, expert in comparative linguistics as she might be, did not understand a thing. She worked morning, noon, and night and she got into a bad mood and Simónides gave her little pats on the back, literally and figuratively. She was only able to decipher the alphabet—the alphabets, because there were five although all of the books (according to Fineschi, who applied the I-don't-know-who reaction to them) were from the same period. I warn you that this *from the same period* for them meant four or five centuries. Finally, they stopped digging around in the hills except to take out the books Veri Halabi said she needed, because things were repeated more or less in all of them and they couldn't carry any more. The girl kept working, the others did what they could or what they felt like, and then I arrived."

He seemed to remember the coffee and he offered it to the others but the only one who accepted was the Albino because Flynn had a glass of whiskey and Cirito drinks little.

"In all this, Marina divided her attention between the prodigious civilization and the skinny monkeys who danced. The day they heard the music for the first time, they almost had heart attacks because they didn't expect it and they went to see what was happening. Armed, just in case. All but Veri Halabi, who from the outset had felt an aversion toward them and who said the music was irritating. And every time she heard it, she shut everything and stayed inside and if she thought she heard something, she covered her ears. Simónides told me that later. By the time I arrived, they were used to the music and the dance and they liked it. Marina told me that now and then, not every day but once in a while and at irregular intervals, without there being any sign or anything happening, they took out sticks, strings, some very simple instruments that she described and that I saw but don't even remember, and some played music and all the others danced. They danced for hours and hours without tiring, the stamina they had was incredible, they were so skinny and sickly, nourished on ground-up worms and water. But they danced sometimes all day, sometimes all night. Have you ever tried to dance a whole night without stopping? Well, they could. They danced in the most complete darkness, without seeing each other, without pushing each other, without falling. Or they danced during the day, what passed for day under the purple sun. Or they danced partly during the day and partly at night. And suddenly, just because, the music stopped and they threw themselves down anywhere looking at who knows what and they did nothing for hours or days. Impressive. I swear to you, it was impressive."

At that point in the evening and in the story, no one thought it necessary to keep drinking anything but Trafalgar did not abandon the electric coffeepot. It was cold and Cirito stood up to turn on the heat while Flynn and the Albino waited and Trafalgar probably thought about the dark days of Anandaha-A.

"I liked the dance, too, as I liked them, although I was unable to sell them anything," he went on when he saw Cirito come in. "And the people in the camp liked it, too. I'm not just saying Marina Solim, who is disposed to like everything, or Lundgren, who learned sintu and that already speaks in favor of the good disposition of any individual, nor the sociologist who accepts what comes and immediately composes a synoptic chart and I don't remember his name but I do recall he passed the hours smoking Craven A's and typing. Everyone liked it and every time they heard music, they went to watch. All save Halabi. The music was sharp, harsh, almost boiling and with a rhythm that if the rockers heard it, they'd commit suicide from envy. It was. Damn, it is not easy to describe a music. It was not inhuman. Look, I think if someone played it at one of those dance clubs, the kids would start dancing happy as can be. That's it. It was a music that transformed everything into music, although Lundgren said it was tragic and, yes, it was tragic. It seemed as if it were the first time you realized that you were alive and that you had been alive long before and maybe you were going to be again but you were going to die at any moment and you had to dance so your legs and arms and hips and shoulders wouldn't get mixed up in a single rigid body, immobile. I thought that was why they danced. Instead of making things, screws or cities or philosophical systems, they danced to recognize and to say that they were alive. I asked Simónides and he told me that was exactly one of his theories about the dance. The others were that the dance was a language, that it was a rite of worship, that it was the memory of something lost. Following on that last, like the sociologist and like Marina Solim, he had asked himself if the inhabitants of this dark and almost dead world might not be the descendants of those who had built and occupied that which now was in ruins. But Veri Halabi had become furious. Violently, inexplicably, and disproportionately furious, Simónides told me, and she had said that to think those brutes belonged to the same race as the owners of the alphabets was almost sacrilegious. They left her in peace because they knew she was having a hard time with the tension of a project that could not be resolved. But not Simónides. The little bald doc was never deceived. At that moment, he didn't know what was going on, he couldn't know that, but he did know something more was cooking there than the self-respect of a beautiful, persnickety expert in comparative linguistics."

"She probably liked the guys who were dancing and didn't want to admit it," said the Albino Gamen.

"Albino, you're a genius," said Trafalgar.

"She liked them?" asked Cirito, very alarmed.

"Liked them?" said Trafalgar. "Now I'll tell you how things happened. The thing that had caught Simónides' attention was that Halabi said the music was irritating and she didn't want to go see what it was that very first time. And she had remained alone in the camp darning stockings, I imagine, or memorizing the fourth chapter of some treatise on comparative linguistics because they hadn't yet found the books. The doctor stored the fact away in his little gossipy brain because that was his occupation: to pay attention to what the others said and did, put it all together, draw conclusions and then have a chat with his victim to explain that they had to work out their frustrations or else another one of the things those guys say. I don't say it's not useful, on the contrary, and the proof is that everything ran smooth as silk, even poor Fineschi, who, apart from drooling on himself when he looked at the little brunette, was reasonably happy. And outside of the work each of them had to do, the dance was the main attraction. The only problem was that there was a performance only seldom. And when there was one, Halabi got nervous and started to close herself in as soon as the music could be heard and the others went to see. And then they found the ruins and all of them set to work like dwarves and she more than any of them. Things were resolving themselves, except for the writing part, and when I arrived the people of Anandaha-A had begun to dance more frequently all the time. When I saw the spectacle, I was left dumbstruck and I think I even dreamt and from then on I didn't miss one. Simónides told me his theories, Marina too, I played sintu with Lundgren (who cheated, if you ask me), I tried my luck like everyone else with a few discreet verbal passes at Halabi, who, if one could pull her away from linguistics and her hatred of the natives, was very sociable and smiling, and I resigned myself to not selling anything, but I stayed."

The dining room was warm and full of smoke and the Albino took off his jacket. Cirito had on an old sweater that was worn through at the elbows, which if Fina saw it, she'd die on us. In the room facing the street the clock struck three but they didn't hear it.

"One time," Trafalgar said, "we spent almost the whole day watching them dance. There were only two musicians, one who blew and another who scraped and beat. All the rest danced. It was an obsession: we could not move from where we were. We went to lunch very late and Marina went to see her and told us Halabi was sleeping shut up in her room. It seemed strange to me, and to Simónides, too, because lately the girl slept very little, crazy as she was with trying to decipher the books. We went back to keep watching the dance and when we were too worn out we went to sleep and they kept dancing and Veri Halabi's room was still closed and the light was off. Simónides peeked in and he told me yes, she was sleeping, but she was very restless. The doctor told me a few things, I don't know why;

maybe because doctors also need someone to listen to them some-times. The next day, in spite of having slept so much, the girl had cir-cles under her eyes down to here and was pale and haggard. I won't say she was ugly, because she had a long way to go for that, but she was less pretty. That day there was no dance. The next day she couldn't take it anymore and she told Simónides that she had dreamed about the texts for hours and hours and Simónides told her of course she did and there was nothing strange about that. He didn't understand her, she said, it was about the texts deciphered and translated. But she said no, it couldn't be, everything was nonsense and she started to become hysterical. Simónides took her to bed, not with libidinous but with therapeutic intent, now that is professional ethics, my God. He talked to her for a while and calmed her down and then she told him that shut up inside and everything, she kept hearing the music and even if she covered her ears she kept hearing the music and she had almost started to dance. And so as not to dance, she lay down and she had fallen asleep immediately and she had dreamt about guess what, you got it, about the music and the people dancing. And as hap-pens in dreams, the people dancing had become the unknown letters of the five alphabets, only in the dream she knew them and she could read them. Simónides told her what anyone would have said: some-times, not often but it does happen, in dreaming one encounters the solution to a problem about which one has thought so much that one can't even see it clearly while awake. But she told him—*she* told *him*, note—he was crazy and he should open the desk drawer, her drawer. The doctor opened it and he found a pile of papers written by Halabi: it was the translation she had dreamt and that, upon waking, she had rushed to record she didn't know why since she was still convinced it was nothing but a nightmare. Simónides didn't manage to read every-thing, unfortunately. He remembered only a few things. There was, for example, the description of a circle."

"The description of what?" burst out Flynn.

"Of a circle."

Flynn tried to pull his leg: "A geometric figure formed by the interior points of a circumference, if I am not mistaken."

"I am sorry to inform you that you are mistaken. I am going to tell you what a circle is according to the protocol of the sense of Anandaha-A."

Here all of them interrupted because no one understood that about *protocol of the sense*. But Trafalgar Medrano didn't know what it meant. Simónides didn't either, and at that moment neither did Veri Halabi. It was in the texts and that was all.

"A circle," said Trafalgar, "is formed in the kingdom when the oil lamp burns out in the perceptible game."

"Just a minute, just a minute," said Flynn. "If in a dark world like that you light a lamp, in certain a way it forms a circle, but it isn't formed when you turn out the light, do we agree?"

"Will you let me finish? I am not explaining anything to you. I am telling you what was in the texts Simónides read, which were the translation Veri Halabi did while dreaming, based on a quintuple alphabet that she did not know."

"What a mess," said the Albino.

"A circle," Trafalgar began again, "is formed in the kingdom when the oil lamp burns out in the perceptible game of every distant precinct. As quartz is unaware of the howl of the wild animal and if it rains on the high grasslands it is improbable that the roots will know, all precincts come in contact at the rough edges until knowledge erases that which has been constructed. Its measure depends not on the rocks but on the torrent."

"And what does that mean?" asked Cirito.

Flynn served himself more whiskey.

"I don't know," Trafalgar said. "Simónides had a theory, he always had theories for everything and I think sometimes he was not mistaken. Almost triumphantly, he told me that Anandaha-A was a world of symbols. I allowed myself to suggest that all worlds function by symbols the way all tricycles function by pedal but he told me there is a big difference between *of* symbols and *by* symbols. It seems to me he's right. And he said that to burn out the oil lamp is to leave the mind blank, to not think of anything, and that this is something that is very easily said but is difficult to do because it is nothing less than the elimination of the conscious to leave room for the unconscious, how's that? The kingdom is the quality, the essence of being human, and the perceptible game is consciousness and every distant precinct is each individual. When the oil lamp is lit, the precincts are far from one another, each one is alone. The part about quartz and the wild animal and the rain and the high grasslands and the roots means, according to Simónides, that although the universe apparently functions divided into infinite parts, or not so infinite, depending how you look, it is all unique and one, indivisible and the same in all of its points. Understand?"

"No."

"Nor I. I'll continue. So, as the universe is one and unique in all of its points, if each individual suspends its consciousness and puts out the oil lamp, everyone meets, they are not alone, they unite and they know everything with no need for and in spite of the great intellectual creations. And knowledge is deeper in proportion to how total each individual's effort is and not how many individuals there are. That would be the part about the measure."

"Ingenious," said Flynn.

"Shit," said Albino, "I don't understand a thing."

Cirito said nothing.

"And so on like that," continued Trafalgar. "There was a text about how to project statues but Simónides didn't know if it was project in the sense of drawing prior to the task of sculpting or project through space. There was also a dialogue between God and man in which of course the only one who spoke was the man. A list of harmful volitions: don't ask me, Simónides didn't know what that was either and if he had a theory he forgot to tell me. Theorems, a pile of theorems. A travel diary. A method for folding but I don't know folding what. And stacks of other things. But all of that was lost. Simónides recorded the little he remembered and somewhere I must have a copy he gave me. Because while he was reading, Veri Halabi had some big attack, she stood up and started to shred papers and she even grabbed the papers Simónides had in his hand and ripped them to bits."

"What a crazy," said the Albino.

"Uh-huh," said Trafalgar, "that is what one thinks every time someone does something one does not understand. But wait a little and tell me afterward if she was crazy. The doc put everything aside and took care of her and he gave her something to let her sleep. He told me there had been no such attack, that simply and unfortunately, at that moment the perceptible game had fully invaded her and she had abandoned the kingdom. I preferred not to ask for explanations but I asked him if it wasn't possible to reconstruct the texts and he told me no, they were confetti and anyway they weren't texts in danger of being lost. I also asked him if he thought they were the concrete translation of the metal books and he looked at me as if I had asked him if he believed two plus two makes four and he told me of course they were. And what can I tell you, the next day Halabi gets up fresh as a daisy and devotes herself to continuing her work on the translation."

"But how?" said the Albino. "Hadn't she already done it and ripped it up? She did it again?"

"No. It was the first time. She didn't want to believe that what she had torn up was the translation and, awake, she worked by putting into operation logic, reasoning, information—which is to say, outside the kingdom, in the perceptible game—now without knowing and without trying to form a circle. Then life goes on as always and nothing's happened here and for two days there are no dances. On the third day, it occurs to Romeo Fineschi Montague to propose that we all go on an outing. An outing on that lousy world, imagine. But of course, if he goes and invites Julieta Halabi Capulet alone, he comes up empty, because she says no. We went. Dalmas, Lundgren, Marina, Simónides, me, Fineschi, Halabi, two other engineers and even the sociologist. Very fun it was not, because as I already told you the natural attractions of Anandaha-A are pitiful. We talked nonsense and Simónides described imaginary monuments and parks in the voice of a tour guide until he got tired because we weren't paying too much attention. The only one who was having a ball was Fineschi, who was talking to Halabi a mile a minute, I imagine about such romantic topics as the degree of saline saturation in the water of the lower Danube. We were on our way back when the music started and Veri

Halabi cried out. It was a cry to stand your hair on end, like a cornered beast, as the science fiction writers say."

"And others who don't write science fiction," Flynn noted.

"I don't doubt it. Apart from science fiction and detective novels, I read nothing but Balzac, Cervantes, and Corto Maltese."

"You'll go a long way with that ridiculous mishmash."

"Ridiculous, how? How? They are among the few that have everything one can ask of literature: beauty, realism, entertainment, what more do you want?"

"Give it up, guys," said the Albino. "Why'd the girl yell?"

"One cries out from pain or fear or surprise," said Flynn. "Less frequently, from happiness. Although I think that was not the case here."

"It was not. She cried out. A long cry that seemed to come up from her heels and that scraped her throat. She stood there a moment planted like a stake with her jaw dropping down to her knees and her eyes like the two of coins and afterward she ran off toward the camp. The music sounded very sharp, urgent, but instead of going to see, we followed her, Fineschi at a trot and the rest walking quickly. Simónides went to see her and he found her sitting on the bed, stupefied. This time she hadn't shut herself in nor did she cover her ears. The good doctor kicked out Fineschi, who was just a pain in the neck trying to talk to her, he looked at her for a while, took her pulse, did all the things quacks do, and left her alone. She didn't bat an eyelid. We were all a little overwhelmed and the music continued and a few went to see. The rest of us stayed and ate. Fineschi paced and smoked a pipe that went out every two minutes. The others came back, they ate and all of us sat down for a kind of dismal after dinner talk. From time to time, Simónides would go to see her and when he came back he said nothing. Then, when we were about to go to bed, she appeared in the doorway. The music continued and the girl started to talk. The catch was we understood nothing. She talked and talked in an unknown language in which there were many more vowels than it would seem there should be. We listened to her without moving and when Fineschi tried to approach her, the good doctor did not let him. She talked the whole night."

"That can't be," said Flynn.

"What do you know? She talked the whole night and we listened to her the whole night. Fineschi cried from time to time. Marina Solim was sitting at my side and she grabbed me by the arm and she didn't let go until her hand cramped up. When it dawned, which is a pretty literary figure to stick into this story because it doesn't dawn there, the little violet sun rises and it is less dark and that's all; when it dawned, the music was still playing and she was still talking. And suddenly she stopped talking but the music did not stop. I was numb and even cold and the others must have been as well but when Veri Halabi went out, we got up and went after her. She walked as if she had to deposit cash at the bank and it was one minute to four, and the rest of us followed behind, toward where the music was. There at the foot of one of the excavated hills, beside the blackish river, the Anandaha-A folk were dancing with so much enthusiasm it seemed as if they had just begun. And Veri Halabi ran and thrust herself among them and danced and while she danced she tore off her clothes and shook her head until her black hair covered her face like all the rest and we could no longer tell her apart. Another hour passed and, crazy with sleepiness and fatigue and with the sense that something more inevitable than death had happened, we retreated to the camp. Simónides and Dalmas had to drag Fineschi, who did not want to leave. We went to bed and we all slept, Simónides last because he went around handing out pills and he gave Montague an injection. I slept for ten hours and was one of the first to wake up. Marina Solim set to making coffee and the sociologist smoked but did not type. Afterwards, Simónides appeared and little by little the others. We drank coffee and ate sausage sandwiches. And the music that had kept playing—and I don't know how, because I slept like a log, but I know it had kept playing all day—the music stopped with the last crumb of food. Fineschi announced that he was going to look for the girl and there we all went again, in procession, but it was useless."

"She wasn't there?" asked the Albino.

"Yes, she was there. At first we didn't see her. The natives had sat down or laid down wherever like always, staring fixedly at some point.

It was hard to pick her out. Now she was dressed in a sack open at the sides and seated in the mud with her legs crossed, between two women and a man, so similar to them, with her eyes very open, without blinking, mute and more beautiful than before because she had become beautiful like the lords of Anandaha-A. She looked straight ahead but she didn't see us. We called her and I was sure we were behaving like a bunch of idiots. She didn't hear us. Simónides grabbed the sociologist and Lundgren and went to get her. I restrained Fineschi. As soon as they put their hands on her, the music started again and everyone stood up and danced, Halabi as well, and dancing they rejected the three men who backed hurriedly out of the whirl and we lost sight of her. In three days we made five more attempts. It was no use. Finally it was Fineschi, and that surprised me, who said we had to admit defeat."

The Albino said can't you see she was crazy and Cirito said who knows and Trafalgar drank more coffee.

"She wasn't crazy," he said. "She had returned to her home, to the circle. Look, if I think about it a lot, I have no alternative than to say yes, she went crazy. But if I remember her dancing, telling us by dancing that we should leave her in peace because she had stopped searching, resisting, studying, thinking, writing, reasoning, accumulating, and doing, I recognize with some satisfaction—a sad satisfaction, because I don't carry that marvel in my blood—that she had crossed the kingdom from end to end and she was swimming fresh and lovely in the torrent. Simónides explained it another way and Marina Solim supported him with very concrete data. The people who danced were in fact the descendants of those who had left the ruins. Anandaha-A knew, perhaps, a yellow, hot star and a clean sky and fertile soil and they manufactured things and wrote poems long before we treated ourselves to the stegosaurus and the scaphites. Perhaps they had jewels, concerts, tractors, wars, universities, candies, sports, and plastic material. They must have traveled to other worlds. And they reached so high and so deep that when the star died, it no longer mattered to them at all. After visiting dead worlds, worlds living or to be born, after leaving their seed on a few of them, after exploring everything and knowing everything, they not only stopped caring about the death of the star, but about the rest of the universe and they had enough with the sense of the circle. They preserved nothing but the music that they danced and that was all Simónides had supposed and much more. We don't know what more but if someone told us, we wouldn't understand. And Veri Halabi recognized her own but the light of the perceptible game prevented her from seeing them and entering the kingdom where there is the possibility of putting out the oil lamp, and torn between the light and the nostalgic urgency of a few of her cells which bore the seal of the Argonauts of Anandaha-A, she hated them. When the light went out by force of the music and she spoke all the words of her race, those she had learned in dreams, she no longer hated them or loved them or anything. It was enough to return."

The Albino says they were all quiet. Even Flynn, who is argumentative and likes to take the opposing side, found nothing to say. When Cirito remarked that Fina had called on the phone to let him know she was staying in Salta another week and they talked about other things and drank more whiskey and Trafalgar more coffee, Flynn admitted that Trafalgar could be right, that the matter, if you thought about it carefully, seemed preposterous, yet he had the impression that it wasn't all that strange. Cirito said:

"I'd like to go to Anandaha-A."

"It's all yours," said the Albino.

"Was Veri Halabi that pretty?" asked Flynn.

"Now she is prettier," said Trafalgar.

Of Navigators

At a quarter to ten, the bell rang. It was a Thursday of one of those treacherous springs that befall us in Rosario: Monday had been winter, Tuesday summer, Wednesday it had gotten dark in the south and hot in the north and now it was cold and everything was gray. I went to answer, and it was Trafalgar Medrano.

"We're sunk," I told him. "I have no coffee."

"Oh, no," he answered. "You won't scare me off so easily. I'm going to buy some."

A short while later he returned with a one kilo packet. He came in and sat at the kitchen table while I heated the water. He said it was going to rain and I said it was lucky we'd had the ligustrinas pruned the week before. The cat came and rubbed herself against his legs.

"What are you doing?" Trafalgar asked her; to me he said, "I don't know how there are people who can live without cats. In the court of the Catholic Monarchs, for example, there were no cats."

I served him the coffee. "What would you know about the court of the Catholic Monarchs?"

"I'm just coming from there," he answered, and he drank half the cup.

"Stop kidding me. How's the coffee?"

"Disgusting," he answered.

I wasn't surprised. Partly because Trafalgar finds all coffee disgusting, unless it's the coffee he makes himself or that made by Marcos in the Burgundy or by two or three other chosen ones in the world;

and partly because I do a few things moderately well, but coffee is not included on the list. The cat climbed up on his lap and half-closed her eyes, considering whether or not it was worthwhile to stay.

"Patience, drink it anyway," and I served him another cup while I let my own get cold. "How did you manage to travel to the 15th century?"

"I don't see why I should travel to the 15th century. Besides, time travel is impossible."

"If you came to shake up my bookshelves, you can be going and leave me the coffee as tribute. I love time travel, and so long as I think it is possible, it is possible."

The cat had decided to stay.

"The coffee is a gift," said Trafalgar. "I am going to explain to you why one cannot travel through time."

"No. I don't want to know. But don't tell me that if you come from the court of the Catholic Monarchs you didn't travel through time."

"What little imagination you have."

That didn't surprise me either. "Very well," I said, "tell me."

And I put the coffee pot on the table.

"Perhaps the universe is infinite," he said.

"I hope so. But there are those who go around saying it isn't."

"I say that because this time I traveled through some very strange places."

That did surprise me. If there is something Trafalgar, accustomed to traveling among the stars, finds strange, it is truly strange.

"If I tell you," he continued, and he served himself more coffee. "Don't you have a larger cup? Thank you. If I tell you that not even the merchant princes go there."

"And who are they?"

"I call them the merchant princes, you can imagine why. They call themselves the Caadis of Caá. They're like the Phoenicians but more sophisticated. I know they don't go there because the last time I was with one of them, I think it was on Blutedorn, I discovered, exchanging itineraries, that they had nothing marked in that sector."

"What is it? Is it dangerous, sinister, all who enter are lost or go crazy or are never seen again?"

He disillusioned me.

"It's too far away. The merchant princes aren't idiots. A lot of expense for questionable profits. I'm not an idiot either, but I am inquisitive and I had plenty of extra money. I had been selling tractors on Eiquen. Did I ever tell you about Eiquen? A little world, all green, that moves very slowly around two twin suns?"

"Spare me Eiquen. How did you end up in the court of Isabel and Fernando?"

"Eiquen is probably a crossroads, or a hinge. Tell me, and if the universe were symmetrical?"

I liked the idea. So did the cat.

"Now you'll see why," said Trafalgar. "I left the tractors on Eiquen, I charged more than you can imagine, and instead of coming back, I kept going. Don't forget I'm inquisitive. I wanted to know what there was farther on, so to speak, and on the way see if I could buy something, because I no longer had anything to sell. And I had cash, and I was tired. It was a long trip. I slept, I ate, I got bored, and I didn't find anything interesting. I was about to turn around when I saw a world that could be inhabited and I decided to land." He looked sadly at what remained of the coffee. "Of one thing I am sure: if my heart didn't fail me that time, it never will."

"Why? What happened?"

"Make more coffee. But put in less water. And don't let it boil. And moisten the coffee first with a few drops of warm water."

"I would like to write my memoirs," I told him, "but I can't bring myself to get started. Someday I'm going to write yours and I'll have my revenge." I began to make more coffee.

The cat must have given him one of her looks because he continued the story: "The world was blue, gray, green. I got closer and as I descended I began to see Europe, Africa, the Atlantic, and for less than a second it occurred to me that I had returned. I don't know if you realize how disconcerting the situation was, to put it mildly. A mountain of awful things went through my mind and I even thought

I had died at some point between Eiquen and Earth. I calmed myself as best I could and went to check and I found it was the third planet in a system of nine. I said, I'm crazy, and I asked for more data and luckily I wasn't crazy nor had I died: the spectrum was not entirely the same. Then I got to looking more calmly and there were little things, a few details that did not coincide. It was a world very similar to this one, almost identical, but it wasn't this one. Don't tell me the situation wasn't looking tempting. I, at least, passed from fear to temptation. I turned around and came this way, I mean, I set off toward the part of that world that resembled this one, if there was one. Because if on that world there existed another Europe, another Mediterranean, another Africa, there had to exist another South America, another Argentina, another Rosario. I was half right. The continent existed, but it was empty as a poor man's pocket, or at least that's how it seemed to me. I even touched down beside the Paraná, the other Paraná, understand. Nothing was missing for it to be a nightmare: I knew where I was but nothing was as it should have been. There was no one, there was nothing. A viper frightened me, I heard a few roars, it was cold, so I lifted off again. It made me sad: a world like ours and wasted. But again I was mistaken. I flew over Europe and it was populated. I landed in Spain. In Castile. It was summer. This coffee is a little better than the other. I'm not saying it's good," he checked me, "it's a little less undrinkable."

"Cretin," I said. "You could be more agreeable with the future author of your memoirs."

He did no more than just barely smile and keep drinking that coffee that according to him wasn't good for much.

"Well, and . . . ?"

"And what?"

"Was that where Isabel and Fernando came out to receive you?"

"No. There was a tremendous uproar, true. Imagine, in Castile in 1492, a machine that comes down from the sky."

"Wait a minute. You really mean to tell me that."

"Don't you see you have no imagination? A world almost identical to this one, understand? Almost identical. The contour of Africa, for example, was different. There were some peninsulas and some rather large archipelagos that don't exist here. And in history, their clock was five centuries behind. Details. There were others, you'll see. If you don't keep interrupting me, of course. There was a big uproar, as I said. I had to wait almost the whole morning for someone in authority to get there, while those who had gathered decided whether to lynch me or canonize me. An unruly troop of soldiers finally came, which did nothing to settle things down. I remained locked in, waiting to see what happened. When I saw the embroidered, empurpled, bedamasked, and bemedalled appear, I opened up and climbed down. I offered explanations. The situation amused me, so I invented a story according to which I was a traveler from some vague region in the east, I had been in Cathay, and there the emperor had given me the flying machine. At first I didn't have much success, but I got all mystical and we finally ended up all on our knees—you can't imagine what that did to my clothes, between the dirt and the heat—giving thanks to the Almighty and to all the heavenly host. I closed up the clunker and activated the security mechanisms: if anyone got too close, they'd receive a kick strong enough to knock over a camel. The next stop was the court, they told me. I won't even tell you what the trip was like, with the heat, the thirst, the horse they gave me, from which a big man-at-arms who didn't take it too well had to dismount (and you already know that very athletic, I am not), but we finally arrived. That very afternoon, I appeared at court."

"Dressed like that, with one of your formal gray suits, shirt and tie?"

"But no. What I wore on the trip could pass for ceremonial attire in Cathay, but in the palace I was saddled with an embroidered blue costume, with lace, that wasn't fastened with buttons but with little ties and that was tight everywhere. All of this without being able to take a bath, which didn't surprise me too much after having smelled the empurpled and bedamasked ones," he sighed, "and without being able to smoke and without being able to drink coffee. When I remember, I wonder how I didn't go crazy for real."

The cat slept, or pretended to sleep, and the coffee got dangerously low.

"It was handy being a foreigner, you know? I was very much a foreigner, they didn't how much, but they believed me foreign enough to excuse my blunders. They gave me an accelerated course in protocol. I didn't understand any of it, but I kept afloat."

"What would you like this chapter to be called? 'My indiscretions at court'?"

"My indiscretions, you'll forgive me, I am going to skip over; we'll go in stages. The city was worthless: it was a maze of narrow, dirty little streets, a few of them cobbled, the majority no. When we passed the suburbs, I began to see important houses with grilles and balconies and statues of saints, but all of them shut up like tombs and the streets were still filthy and narrow until they opened into a few that were wider. Not a tree, not a plant, not a weed. Burros, horses, dogs, cows, chickens, but not a single cat. An infernal noise, that's true. It seemed as if everyone was yelling, they were all arguing and fighting. I suppose I should have felt myself important, but I felt ridiculous and it wasn't fun anymore, not fun at all. The soldiers went ahead, scattering the onlookers who moved aside but came back like flies and more than one received a blow to the face with the flat of the blade. With all that we advanced so slowly I thought we would never arrive. And then we arrived. The palace was almost as dirty as the streets, but more luxurious. I saw a few things that reconciled me to the trouble I was taking on account of my curiosity: tapestries, carved tables, pictures, grilles, and a black-eyed beauty who couldn't have been more than fifteen years old, wearing an enormous dress, somewhere between orange and brown, with a rigid lace collar."

The cat stretched, yawned, she stood up on Trafalgar's bony knees, and she lay back down with her head facing the other way. Trafalgar waited until the process was completed and petted her behind the ears.

"Doña Francisca María Juana de Soler y Torrelles Abramonte."

"Panchita to her closest friends," I remarked. "Among whom you eventually counted yourself, I'll bet anything."

"Get out. She was married to a big man of the court. One of those smelly old men who look fat but they're really thin with a belly, bowlegged, stuttering, with no more than two or three rotten teeth in his mouth, full of wrinkles, of snot, and of hair in the most inappropriate places. And she, unfortunately, was no more than fifteen."

"Why unfortunately? What more did you want?"

"For her, I'm saying. Do you know I almost brought her with me? I must be crazy."

"I have always maintained something like that."

"I caught just a glimpse of her that afternoon and only because she leaned out to look. Keep in mind that I was the star of the day. And of the month and the year, no exaggeration. But she looked at me as much as she pleased and I knew she was looking and she knew that I knew. The others put me in a salon, more tapestries, more black carved furniture, more pictures, crosses, kneelers and grime, and they offered me an uncomfortable armchair, a work of art but uncomfortable, and a bowl with water and a napkin. I moistened my fingertips, trying to imagine I was taking a shower, but I regret to inform you that I am not very good at autosuggestion. I remained seated and then they all moved away a little and then the dance began."

"They received you with a dance?"

"Don't be an idiot. I'm speaking metaphorically. And you should know that in the court of the Catholic Monarchs there was no place for such frivolities. Keep in mind, they were extremely busy expelling the Moors, expelling the Jews, discovering America and all that."

"Stop, stop, America how?"

Trafalgar has infinite patience. When he wants to.

"What year did I tell you."

"You said five centuries behind."

"To be exact, I told you 1492."

"Jeez!"

"Exactly."

And without his asking, I put more water on to heat. The cat purred under her breath, not like Doña Francisca María Juana I-don't-know-what, but silently, the way she does.

"The dance, metaphorically, began. Which is to say that a few sourpusses dressed in black examined me. There was also a lousy little friar to whom I didn't attach any importance, and I'll tell you right now that was a mistake. I don't know how it didn't catch my attention that alongside so many big shots they let in a common, garden-variety little priest in an old habit who was always looking somewhere else, as if he understood nothing. But keep in mind that I was disoriented. No, the thing no longer seemed fun to me, but it was exciting. That's when I thought that the universe is infinite and symmetrical and don't tell me it can't be because it can. And I also thought I had come across a good substitute for time travel. Too bad I ruined it."

"I know. You told them the truth and they didn't believe you and they delivered you to the Inquisition and Doña María Francisca saved you and the husband found out and."

"But you're crazy, how am I going to tell them the truth? And her name was Doña Francisca María Juana de Soler y Torrelles Abramonte, so you know. No, I didn't tell them the truth. They knew a lot of protocol and a lot of catechism, but I have read something of history and geography and I had a five hundred year advantage. It may not be much, but it was enough. When I saw them, I was on the point of standing up to greet them and I even thought about making a bow, look, not very deep, but sufficiently courtly. And right then I thought about it and said to myself, they can drop dead, what they want to do is screw me, for sure, and the best thing will be to bully them from the outset. I put on my best Voltairian face."

"You don't look like Voltaire, you look like Edmundo Rivero, only handsome."

"Much appreciated. So I looked at them arrogantly, like a know-it-all, and they greeted me and I did not even answer: I half-closed my eyes, I barely nodded my head and I waited. They didn't beat around the bush. They wanted to know, and if I did not tell them or if I lied they would ascertain the truth by such means as they deemed necessary, first, whether I was an envoy of the Evil One; second, whether it was true that I came from Cathay; third, whether they could, following exorcism, blessing, Masses and other nonsense, visit the flying carriage; fourth, what the hell I wanted; fifth, if I planned to stay and live in Castile; and sixth and lastly, what my name was."

"A very thorough survey. What did you tell them?"

"I gave them a speech that lasted about a half an hour and which impressed everyone save for the lousy little friar. To begin I recalled Suli Sul O Suldi, the daughter of a farmer on Eiquen, blessed be her soul for various reasons and blessed be her body for various other reasons, who had given me an ornament that I wore around my neck. It was made of a metal similar to gold but heavier and harder, very elaborately worked and of a size we'll call respectable—some day I'm going to show it to you, I am sure you will like it. The important thing is that it is in the form of a cross. I took it out, exchanged my know-it-all expression for one of infinite sadness with a touch of the school principal's authority and I asked them if they could believe that an envoy of the Evil One would wear that over his heart. First point in my favor. Regarding Cathay, I mixed a sophomore's notions of geography with Marco Polo's voyages and I chalked up the second score. And they could visit my flying carriage and the exorcisms didn't need my authorization; rather, I said, it was a request, a demand on my part, because since it was the gift of infidels, I was a little worried. Three for me. And so on in that fashion: I wanted nothing, I did not aspire to the goods of this world, but I would like to render homage to their majesties. It was possible I would settle in Castile, the land from which my ancestors had come, but as I was an unrepentant traveler, sometimes I would go to travel the world, never forgetting to bring back part of the marvels I encountered to donate to the most illustrious religious orders of the country. By that time, those guys were about to pee themselves and the little friar kept looking into the distance with a wooden rosary between his fingers and I thought, what an asshole and it turns out the asshole was me."

"And what did you tell them you were called?"

"I told them my name, what did you want me to say? Anyway, Trafalgar wasn't going to mean anything to them until three hundred years later, if there was going to be a battle of Trafalgar and an Admiral Nelson. I decorated it a little, granted: I put a *de* before the Medrano, I added two names and my old lady's maternal surname, Hispanized. Turned out better than made to order. The proof is that the sour faces sweetened, and as I knew I had them in my pocket, I stood up and condescended to chat familiarly with all of them. After a while they informed me that they would house me in the palace, which was an honor, and I regretted it because I was sure there were no baths, as indeed there were not; I consoled myself thinking that at that moment there weren't any, I won't even say baths, not even a toilet or a miserable septic tank in all of Castile, so I put on an enthusiastic expression."

"In the end it turns out you're not brazen faced, as I believed, but rubber faced."

"It depends. When they left me alone, which means they left me with three servants who were running all over the place and as far as I could tell didn't do anything, I stretched out on a bed that had a bunch of curtains but was very comfortable and I went to sleep."

"How you can sleep in the midst of the things that happen to you is something that I do not understand."

"If I couldn't fall asleep as necessary, things would have stopped happening to me a while ago."

"Should I make more coffee?"

"I was about to ask what you were waiting for. About two hours later, they came to wake me with a good bit of to-do and they brought me those clothes I told you about, all on top of a cushion. There was even a hat, my God. And a sword. The shoes were both for the same foot and I almost let out a yell but I realized in time that it would be many more years before they made them different. I put everything on and thus I went into the throne room or whatever it was."

"Go on, go on, what was it like?"

"A bore, full of announcements, marches, countermarches, blows of the staff and I don't know what. And they all had a stench of goat that would knock you over. And it was hot. And I was already up to here with the Spanish monarchy."

"Castile and Aragon."

"Whatever. The protocol, I don't even remember the protocol, but do you want me to tell you something? Isabel was quite pretty, not as pretty as Doña Francisca María Juana de Soler y Torrelles Abramonte, and older, but pretty. In the face, at least; as to the rest, I have no idea, with all those infected rags. Fernando had a tic and opened and closed his eyes every five seconds. If he'd been one of the boys at the café, they'd have called him Neon Sign, bet on it. And guess who was at the side of the throne?"

"The lousy little friar."

"Exactly."

We heard a hissing in the garden and there was a crack of thunder but the cat was unperturbed.

"It's raining," Trafalgar said. "Didn't I tell you? The combination of rain and coffee reminds me of the feast of the lightning bolts on Trudu. Do you know what Trudu is?"

"No, but I imagine it's somewhere where it always rains and where coffee comes out of the faucets instead of water."

"Trudu? No. To begin, there are no faucets and to continue, it rains once every ten years."

"Great for growing rice."

"Although you might not believe it, they grow rice, though of course not the rice you know. And in addition, the rain."

"I don't care!" I yelled so loud that the cat opened her eyes and even made a comment under her breath. "Keep Trudu, it's my gift to you, but go on with your presentation at court and with the little friar and with Isabel and with Fernando."

"Fernando you can file away without a pang of conscience. Now, Isabel," he smiled again and two smiles from Trafalgar in a single morning is a record, "was very pretty, yes, but she was a real man with a pair of brass balls. You could see it in her eyes and in the fact that although she had a more than acceptable mouth, she could narrow it until it resembled a stab wound. And her shoulders well back, her neck straight and her hands strong. I said, this girl is going to cause me trouble."

"And the little priest?"

"There you have it, the little priest was the one who gave me the trouble although for the moment he was lying low. That time it did catch my attention that he always appeared at the important meetings, that he was so close to the throne and that nobody seemed to pay him any attention. I went so far as to think he surely wasn't what he seemed, but with as much care as I had to take with what I said and did, I left it for later. Don't forget what I was in the middle of. I had to recount my adventures again, silently invoking Marco Polo, Edgar Rice Burroughs, Italo Calvino, and the annals of geography. It turned out very well: they were all hanging on what I said, they were scared when they were supposed to be scared and they laughed when they were supposed to laugh. I saw Doña Francisca María Juana again."

"De Abramonte Soler y Torrelles."

"De Soler y Torrelles Abramonte, you would cut a sorrier figure than I at court, and I saw the old fart who alternately drooled and snorted. Fernando closed and opened his eyes more continuously all the time and wiggled his nose and possibly his ears. Isabel, in contrast, went so far as to soften her mouth and smile at me and it seems that was the height of privilege. And speaking of privileges, I even ate with their majesties that night, which is saying a lot."

"How was the food?"

"Rather meager. Frugal, which sounds more elegant. And better we not speak of their majesties' table manners. Nor of mine, because without forks there's not much one can do in the way of delicate gestures. The little priest wasn't there, thank goodness. But it was there that they told me about Columbus. By then I had already begun to get used to it all and I felt like a little picture in a history text, but that was too much. And more so when I asked if I could meet him and they told me they expected him the next day at court, when he was going to inform them of how the preparations for the expedition were going. I don't know if it was the food which, in addition to being scarce was a sticky, lumpy mess, or the prospect of meeting him personally even if he wasn't the real one, which in fact he was, but I had a sort of weight in my stomach. Luckily the supper didn't last long because it seemed one had to go to bed early. Which I did. Early and in company."

Another thunder clap, more hisses, more coffee.

"As I had already suspected that would be the case, or more probably just because that was what I wanted, I got rid of the servants, I took off that ridiculous outfit, I chewed on my nails thinking about coffee, cigarettes, a book by Chandler, Jackaroe, television, anything, and I waited. She came around midnight, when I had already put out the candles but I still didn't want to admit defeat and go to sleep. I learned the old man had a post that obliged him to go out to inspect the barracks or the markets or I don't remember what before dawn, and so he went to bed at six in the evening, got up at eleven-thirty, locked her in, and left."

"And how did she get out?"

"Do you think the key has been invented that will keep a woman locked up? Give me a break. And she had accomplices, of course. She left as lookout an old woman who, next to the husband, looked like Miss World, and she came straight to my bed."

He was quiet.

"Trafalgar, don't get discreet on me."

"This time, I'm sorry, but yes, I am going to be discreet."

"And how am I going to write your memoirs?"

"I'll probably tell you one day. The one thing I'll tell you is that I was not the first one to put horns on the old man. Rather than annoy me—you know I am a confessed libertine and for that reason I like them chaste and modest—it made me happy, because it was only right the girl have her revenge for the pawing of such a husband. She knew how to get even, I assure you. At dawn, the old woman knocked on the door and she went off in a rush. I ask, do you think you're in Castile in the 15th century that you don't make more coffee?"

"So much coffee is going to ruin your appetite."

"Bet you it won't. I'll treat you to lunch."

"No, my treat."

"We'll see."

"What do you mean, we'll see? You'll stay to lunch and that's that. Anyway, go on."

"I spent a cushy morning, more desperate by the minute for a smoke and a cup of coffee, but cushy. Surrounded by Lady Bigshot and Mr. Bigwig, relating my adventures, strolling through the palace and through the gardens, which were worthless. After lunch, I had another audience with Isabel, who sent for me. Once again, there was the little priest. As always alone and with an unhappy face but well placed. I had forgotten about him, go figure, what with the night I had passed, but he was beginning to worry me and maybe it was because of that he didn't take me by surprise—or at least if I lost, I lost without making a fool of myself. We had a long conversation, Isabel and I, about philosophy, religion, politics, and—hold on—mathematics. I defended myself like a lion. Do you remember what I told you about her? All the same, I had underestimated her. Intelligent, but very intelligent. And in addition, informed about everything there was to know at that moment in time. And hard as a usurer's heart. I don't know if I racked up so many points in my favor, but as for a tie, we were tied."

"Because you are very cultured, don Medrano."

"It didn't do me any harm to know a few things, because the little priest was there for a reason."

"I already know. He was from the Inquisition."

"Worse. With that five-century lead, I was able to perform well and I was in agreement with her on everything, making out as if I were offering my own reasons although my guts were twisting at the outrageous things I was saying. When we were heatedly justifying the Reconquista, Columbus was announced."

"Oh!"

"What's wrong?"

"I'm moved."

"I was too."

"What was he like, what did he say to you, what did he do?"

"He was crazy."

That took my breath away, but then I thought better. "Of course," I said. "All of them were crazy."

"All of who?"

"People like Columbus. Like Hector, like Gagarin, like Magellan, Bosch, Galileo, Dürer, Leonardo, Einstein, Villon, Poe, Cortés, Cyrano, Moses, Beethoven, Freud, Shakespeare."

"Stop, stop, you're going to drive the whole human race crazy."

"I wish. You already know what I think of sanity."

"At times I agree with you. But I tell you he was crazy: he was going to do anything, anything, deceive, kill, grovel, bribe, swindle, whatever it took, to get himself to sea with his three little boats. Which were four, there: the *Santa María*, the *Pinta*, the *Niña*, and the *Alondra*."

"Go on, seriously?"

"Seriously. There were details, I already told you. And there, thinking about the little boats and about what those poor wretches were going to have to go through, the big idea occurred to me. Jeez, I'm a sap."

"What idea? Oh, Trafalgar, what did you do?"

"I changed the course of history, nothing more than that. I didn't realize it at the moment: I just felt sorry for him. I admired him, I was a little afraid of him, not from distrust like with the little priest but because of the heroic, the agonized aspect of the man, but above all I felt pity. Dangerous thing, pity. I thought, poor guys, why should they suffer months at sea, dying of hunger, superstition, and scurvy, if I can carry them to America in half an hour?"

"Fantastic. Of course, how could you not think that?"

"Yes. Of course, I couldn't say it directly; or rather, I suspected that since the little priest was right there, the smartest way was not to say it directly. So I asked for permission to see the ships and it was graciously granted by her majesty. I abbreviate: I spent two more days as a wealthy idler and two more nights as the lover of Doña Francisca María Juana de Soler y Torrelles Abramonte, and on the third day, we went to Palos de Moguer. As the little priest lived more or less tied to Isabel's apron strings, he did not come with us, to my relief."

"The ships, what were the ships like?"

"If the ones that discovered America here were like those, I don't know how they made it. The Admiral took me to see all of them inside and out. He was already Admiral. And Viceroy and Governor General of the lands he was going to discover and he was entitled to a tenth of the riches he was going to find. As I told you, I felt sorry for him and for that reason I was more convinced than ever that I had to take them. I proposed it to him over a big bottle of wine, you can't imagine what good wine, but I missed coffee, and even though he already knew everything about me and about my flying carriage from Cathay, he didn't want to enter the chute. He didn't have a lot of enthusiasm for the idea, and he went on about Ptolemy and Pliny and about the Imago Mundi, about astronomy, about cosmography, and about how to reach Cipango from the west. Prester John was mixed up with the quadrants, Eneas Silvio with Kordesius' navigation tables. He spoke well of Garci Fernández and ill of Fray Juan Pérez and both well and ill of the king of Portugal and well of Isabel. I kept insisting on taking him to America, I mean to say to Cipango in my flying carriage, and he wasn't saying yes. Then we returned to court and there I laid out my intentions and the little priest didn't look at me even once. It took Isabel three seconds to recognize the advantages of a lightning expedition. Fernando didn't speak, I don't know why. And the little priest, not a peep. The Admiral still wasn't convinced: he put up a thousand objections and I refuted them one by one. I thought he didn't want me to steal the glory of the voyage but it wasn't that, since he didn't know if there was going to be glory or not. I knew, but he didn't. And I don't know that what he wanted above all would be the glory; what he wanted was to prove he was right. I finally put myself under his command and self-designated myself pilot of the carriage. But my feints had little importance once Isabel had decided in favor."

"Then America was not discovered on the 12th of October, 1492."

"Of course not, not there. We discovered it the 29th of July, 1492. But first we had to pass through the inquisitorial ordeals, with inspections, canticles, incense, and Masses. And you can't imagine the farewell of Doña Francisca María Juana de Soler y Torrelles Abramonte, who believed the monsters of finis terras were going to devour me, poor thing. She had a very alert little mind but she was very ignorant, what do you expect?"

He daydreamed for a bit about Doña Francisca María and the rest and I went to empty the ashtray, waiting for him to snap out of it.

"We put the crews of the four little boats in the clunker."

"Did they fit?"

"Didn't I tell you I had sold five hundred tractors on Eiquen? Five hundred nineteen. There was room to spare. The fellows were scared to death and they prayed, or else they made out to be tough guys, but they had all gotten pale. And all around, enduring the midday heat because I wanted to reach America in the morning: the monarchs, the court, the clergy, the army, and the commoners. I had explained to them that it wouldn't do to get too close, but it was a struggle to get them to move away until, when I saw their curiosity was stronger than the soldiers, I turned on the engines and they backed up like sheep. Inside, a deathly silence. Of course when we lifted off, the yelling started. Thank goodness there was a fantastic guy, Vicente Yáñez, captain of one of the little boats, and two or three thugs too stupid or too dangerous to be afraid, the kind it's better not to meet late at night around Ayolas and Convención, who threatened to tear all of them to pieces if they didn't stop making such a fuss. I flew low, over the sea, with all the peepholes on transparent so they would miss nothing. But I don't remember anything about the voyage. On the pretext of driving, I closed myself in to drink coffee and smoke, at last. The only thing I lacked was the newspaper. If the sourpusses saw me there, they'd definitely turn me over to the Inquisition."

I thought about an America discovered by a hundred bearded and illiterate slobs, a lunatic, and a man from another world aboard an interstellar ship: insanity is a great sanity, as Bernard Goorden says.

"We took forty-five minutes because I went slowly," said Trafalgar. "At ten to nine in the morning, we landed in San Salvador because I had illusions of respecting history, as if with that little piece of verisimilitude I could repair what I had done. The Admiral and Yáñez could hardly believe we were already on the other side of the world and between the three of us we had a huge job making the others understand and that's even though they'd seen the coasts and the ocean. We disembarked, we took possession, there were speeches and prayers and while the Admiral wept and wrote reports, Yáñez and I traversed the place and we went into the sea. We hunted, we fished, we ate, and in the evening I took them around the sea of the Antilles which they also call Caribe. We spent two days in Cuba and three in Haiti. As there were no remains of ships, we did not build forts. On the fifth day, Yáñez and I between us herded everyone together, because the Admiral, obsessed with his demonstrations of Cipango from the west, wasn't good for much, and I took them on a trip around the world."

"Poor Magellan."

"Don't even talk about it. That is among the least of my worries. Although I suppose that when I came back home, the puzzle I left will have tended to put itself back together all on its own. A tricky puzzle. I not only went around the world as close to the ground or the water as I could, but I went up and up until I showed them all that yes, their world was round and, by the way, that it was a jewel no one deserved and, also by the way, that where we'd been was not Cipango but America, although I did not say America. They had already stopped being afraid and the disorders now were of another kind. Sanitary, to tell the truth. But we returned to Castile from the east and they received us in the palace and there were celebrations that, added to the horns Doña Francisca María Juana de Soler y Torrelles Abramonte and I between us put on her husband, left me exhausted."

"And the little priest?"

"He was around, as always. But I began to watch him and I learned (without asking, because instinct told me it was not advisable to make inquiries and I have a great respect for instinct, which has gotten me out of more than one), I learned who the little priest was."

"You'll forgive me, but I'm not very strong in history."

"I'll loan you a biography of Doña Isabel and you'll see. But anyway, it's getting late and we have to decide about lunch."

It must have been true that it was late, because the cat was wide awake.

"To continue screwing up history, we made five more trips: we took settlers; not conquistadors, notice, settlers. We took animals, plows, furniture, ships, teachers, physicians, chroniclers, bricklayers, blacksmiths, cabinetmakers, everything. Granted, as few soldiers as possible. Priests I had to take a lot of, more than would have been necessary and advisable."

"So, there, that's what the conquest became?"

"I don't know what it became because I had to leave in a rush. The only thing I know is that I slid glory and honors toward the

Admiral's side, although some fell to me despite my efforts, and I suggested the placement of cities to be founded and I even drew the street plans with what I remembered of each one. Perhaps there, if they have already begun to exist and if they will continue existing, Buenos Aires, Lima, La Habana, Santiago, New York, Quito, are my work—indirectly, but mine. Brazil and all of North America, of this I'm sure, are already half colonized by Castile and Aragon. Do you see what I did?"

"Are you sorry?"

"No."

"What do you mean, no?"

"Well, no, I'm telling you, no. A little uneasy, but not sorry. Uneasy because I don't know who is going to invent the telephone and who will win the Second World War, and because I don't know to what side other factors will trend that, if you think about it, are by no means insignificant: Mayas, Aztecs, Incas on one side, to recall only the most important. Portugal, England, France on the other. England above all. What do you think my queen's namesake will do in her turn?"

"You should have stayed and continued tangling things up, at least to be sure everything was going to be completely different."

"You think so? I don't. In the first place, even if I had wanted to stay, which I did not, it would have taken half a lifetime at least, and I wouldn't have been able to, either."

"Thanks to the little priest."

"You have no imagination, but you hide it. Thanks to the little priest. And in the second place, tangling things too much would have done nothing other than eliminate the hope that within five hundred years there might be, there, another Trafalgar Medrano who is probably inquisitive and comes here and sticks his foot in it and changes the course of history which, given how it's going up to now, wouldn't be a bad thing at all."

My heart was about to fail me, too. A woman with the same name as me, would she have a sewer cat with the airs of a princess? Would she sit down in five centuries in her kitchen to listen to the account of a journey that a man named Trafalgar Medrano had made to a green and blue world in a system of nine surrounding a star on the other side of an infinite universe, symmetrical and terrifying?

"I'm going to drink a little coffee, too," I said.

The cat jumped to the ground. And would that woman ask herself if five centuries before there had been a woman who?

"Give her something to eat, she's hungry," said Trafalgar.

"Be quiet," I answered. "Let me think."

I gave some ground beef to the cat and I gave Trafalgar his coffee and I took mine, which was too hot.

"I was there two months," he said. "Time enough so that between us, my flying carriage and I could begin to colonize an entire continent. Autumn was coming to Castile and Aragon and it was spring here, I mean there, you understand me, when on a morning a little like this one but more miserable, upon leaving my rooms, I encountered the little priest. I realized he had been waiting for me and it smelled bad. Not the little priest but what was coming at me. The little priest was one of the few immaculate types to be found at court. His habit or cassock or whatever that's called was very worn and shiny at the elbows and even mended, but it didn't knock you over with the smell. It didn't have a smell. Nor did Doña Francisca María Juana de Soler y Torrelles Abramonte: and like her there were a few that didn't smell. Not that they washed; it would be a question of glands, I imagine.

"Fine, but the little priest?"

"I already told you he didn't smell."

"Don't be difficult. What did he want?"

"That I go, what else would he want? The little priest had his aspirations. He had favored the Admiral's plans not because he thought it was possible to reach Cipango from the west, and it goes without saying he didn't even dream there was another continent in the west, but rather just in case. That jerk could get to be a good player of sintu, combative style. What he wanted was power, and hidden power, which is as satisfactory as the other kind and much less dangerous."

"But if he already had it, why didn't he just stay calm?"

"Power, not only in Castile and Aragon, but in all possible worlds. Behold the height of humility and disinterest. And there, I disturbed him. Because he had limited himself to embroidering intrigues, but I had done important and visible things. I had not only favored the expansion of the realm, and a heck of an expansion, but had acted with supernatural efficiency. Small-minded, unconvinced little souls, like his, feel very poorly when they have to look head on at the supernatural."

"I will never understand the thirst for power."

"You're a little dull, there's nothing to be done. There in the corridor he spoke to me for the first time. He had a little voice just like the cassock: old and mended. He wished me good morning, although it was no longer the hour for good morning, and he asked if I did not believe true wisdom consisted in using the strength of the adversary to one's own benefit. I was not ready for roundtables at that hour, without breakfast and after a rather agitated night, but I had to know what he had up his sleeve and I said yes, in certain cases that could be a correct attitude. He smiled and he told me that observing my schemes, that's how he said it, observing my schemes, he had done precisely that. I began to walk toward where I knew there was something to eat, and he at my side. And then he told me that he had to warn me he no longer needed me. As I did not answer him, he let fly this: 'The moment has arrived for you to go back where you came from, Señor de Medrano.' I stopped right there and told him I would decide that. 'Ah, no, no, no,' he said, and he explained that if I did not leave immediately, he would denounce as an adulteress Doña Francisca María Juana de Soler y Torrelles Abramonte, an adulteress who maintained carnal relations with a subject of Satan. I realized the guy held all the aces and that I had had it, because if he could demonstrate that, and he could, everything we had done would collapse, but I tried to fight a little more. Useless. The little priest may have worn a mended habit but for my part, I think he had money hidden in his mattress: he had bought my servants and a few of those who had sailed with me on the voyages. I not only went to bed with a married woman but I drank strange black potions and breathed fire from mouth and nose when I was alone. With those witnesses, and a few others he could always obtain with a little money or a lot of fear of hell, the Inquisition was going to be satisfied. I surrendered and asked what he wanted. He wanted me to go, that was all. If I returned that very day to the infernos from whence I had come, he would not move a finger to ruin me nor to bring down the conquest, I mean, the colonization, because that was not in his interest. 'And she?' I asked him. He didn't care a bit about her. As I told you, it wasn't the first time she frolicked with another, and for the little priest, who knew all about it, morals and right living interested him much less than pulling the strings behind the throne. So I left."

"Too bad."

"I don't know. It was a good moment to disappear. The Admiral was no longer going to die poor and abandoned but instead covered with glory and honors and gold. No one was going to kill or get himself killed looking for Eldorado, and all of America was going to speak Spanish some day."

"Are you sure?"

"No, of course not, but I can give myself the luxury of believing so. So I invented at top speed an expedition to Australia to see what could be done in those parts, I thought seriously about putting Doña Francisca María Juana de Soler y Torrelles Abramonte into the clunker as contraband and decided not to, I said so long to everyone and expect me back at teatime and bye-bye sweetie and I left. The one who wanted at all costs to go to Australia with me was Yáñez, but as he was in charge of a government in the new world, I made him see that his part was much more important and he stayed. And she will have cried until she found my replacement and I will have passed into legend as the hero swallowed by the unknown and the little priest will secretly sit on the throne that governs a whole continent."

We were quiet, Trafalgar and I. Afterward I went to see if it was still raining and, yes, it was still raining, but it was starting to clear up to the south. The cat went out to the garden, investigated the climate question, and came back in with wet paws and I protested. Trafalgar remained seated at the kitchen table in front of an empty cup.

"On the trip, I had time to think a lot of nonsense," he said while I searched the refrigerator. "I hope the little priest has gotten what he wanted and doesn't pick on her. And that the old fart has died of black plague. And that Yáñez is Viceroy of North America. And that someday, well, you know."

"Uh-huh," I said. "What do you prefer? Kidneys in white wine with rice, or noodles in browned butter and a liver steak with parsley?"

A decision for five hundred years from now is no joke:

"Kidneys," he said.

The Best Day of the Year [1]

"Hey," said Trafalgar Medrano. "You don't greet your friends anymore?"

"And what are you doing here?" I asked him.

Since I'd had to go downtown, I had run to the public library to see if I might meet Francisco. Who wasn't there.

"What does one come to a library for?" Trafalgar said. "Not to play cards, right?"

I just didn't expect to meet Trafalgar in the library. And it's not that he isn't a good reader. He is, somewhat chaotically. Although he insists there is a logical rigor—implacable he says—in combinations like Sophocles-Chandler, K.-Eternauta, and Mansfield-Fray Mocho.

And when we left, of course, he invited me for coffee.

"Around the corner here," I began.

"No," said Trafalgar. "Let's go to the Burgundy."

We walked four blocks almost without speaking, hurrying amidst the hurrying people, and we went into the Burgundy. Marcos gave us a smile and came over.

"Coffee," said Trafalgar, unnecessarily.

Marcos gave me a look between sorry and mocking: they don't serve soft drinks at the Burgundy.

"Well," I said, "coffee. But small and weak."

Trafalgar sighed an indignant *it is and it isn't* and set a packet of unfiltered cigarettes on the table.

---

1 In truth, this story belongs to my son Horacio. That I have written it is no more than chance and the reader will please overlook that detail.

"What were you reading at the library?" I asked.

He took a piece of paper out of his pocket, unfolded it, and read: "Mulnö, *Tres Ensayos sobre el Tiempo*. *Times Time*, by Woods. And *Realité et Irréalite du Temps*, L'Ho."

"Don't tell me. What did you make of all that?"

"That nobody knows a damn thing about time."

Marcos came over and left the cups, a big one for Trafalgar and a small one for me, on the table. And two glasses of cold water. I drank half my water because I wasn't very enthusiastic about the prospect of the coffee.

"I don't know what you want to go investigating time for. It seems to me the best one can do with time is fill it up and let it pass."

"Yes, but what if time were a thing and not a dimension? And if in fact it didn't pass?"

"I don't understand," I said.

"Me, neither."

"So resign yourself and go to the public library to read the Greek lyrics, like Francisco. Anyway, doctors don't understand why people get sick or why they get well and electricians don't understand electricity and mathematicians don't understand zero. Also, why do you want to understand time?"

"Just curiosity," and he fell quiet but he didn't fool me.

The Burgundy is a quiet place, thank goodness. And Trafalgar is a quiet guy. Through the door's twelve beveled glass rectangles one could see people pass by and one wondered why they didn't remain still. Marcos came over with another double coffee because Trafalgar had drunk the first in one swallow, hot as it was and bitter, the way he likes it.

"Marcos," I said, "some day I am going to write a story with you and the Burgundy in it."

"Please, ma'am, no. What if the bar gets fashionable on me and fills up with people?"

"Unlikely. At most, my friends and my aunts will start coming."

"All right then, but, just in case, don't publish it," and he left.

"You could," said Trafalgar, "write a story with each one of my trips."

"Not even if I was crazy," I answered. "In the first place, stories proposed by other people never work: stories choose one, one does not choose stories. And in the second place, your stories are always the same: a bunch of strange things happen to you, you throw yourself, generally successfully, at the prettiest one around there, you earn piles of dough, and what do you spend it on? On bitter coffee and black cigarettes and Pugliese records. Why don't you buy yourself the latest model Mercedes or go to Europe to live large?"

"A remise taxi is more comfortable and you don't have to pay for insurance or a garage. And I go to Europe from time to time. But it doesn't interest me much."

"Of course. Between Freiburg and Anandaha-A, you pick."

"Freiburg," he jumped in. "But if you ever get to see the cathedrals, they're not exactly cathedrals, but anyway, made out of paper that isn't exactly paper, on Tippanerwade III, the Gothic will seem like a caricature to you. And beside the builders of mausoleums."

"Which are not exactly mausoleums."

"They are. Beside the mausoleum builders of Edamsonallve-Dor, the Egyptians were a herd of subnormals, believe me."

"Is that where you've been now?"

"No. It's been three months or so since I've traveled. I came back from Karperp and I spent all this time being lazy."

"What you might have sold on Karperp, I don't even want to consider."

"Musical instruments. Strings, no winds or percussion. And I bought tons of wood from them."

"Poor Karperpianos."

"They're not called Karperianos. They're called Neyiomdavianos."

I thought he was pulling my leg, but he said, "It's a system of thirteen around a star called Neyiomdav, see? Each one of the thirteen has a different name, they're not called Neyiomdav I, Neyiomdav II, and so on, but rather like here, each world has its name, but those who live there go by the name of the star."

"Those of the thirteen worlds?"

"Only two are inhabited. Karperp, where I had an order for violins, lutes, guitars and zithers and violas and all that, and Uunu, which I didn't know was inhabited."

"How did you not know?"

"No one had told me anything. But after delivering the instruments and while loading the wood—remind me to give you a box made of estoa wood that will hold cigarettes or buttons or those things you women like to keep in boxes. Very fine, like a spider's web, but you can't break it even with an axe. And it doesn't burn, either."

"It won't be wood, then. And thank you, I will certainly remind you."

"It's wood. You're welcome. While loading the wood I spent a few days at the home of a friend who lives on the shores of a river in which one can swim, sail, and fish."

"You neither swim nor sail nor fish."

"I don't dislike swimming. Fishing and sailing don't interest me. But now and again, I do like to stretch out in the sun and do nothing. He was the one who mentioned Uunu, in passing. And I was intrigued because he didn't seem to want to offer much explanation. He only told me that they didn't go there because it was hard to recover afterwards. I asked him if it was insalubrious, and he told me that on the contrary, it was a very pleasant place, with a splendid climate, nice people, landscapes *a piacere* and comfortable lodging. I didn't insist because discretion is a virtue everywhere and I assumed Karperp was no different."

Marcos walked past our table because more people had come in, and he left Trafalgar another full cup. I made no move to order more coffee, though my cup was miserably empty.

"As you'll imagine," he continued, "right then I decided to go to Uunu and see what there was to buy. So a week later, with the clunker filled to the top (the Neyiomdavianos are laid-back, they don't hurry even if someone's about to slit their throats, and it took them ten days to load everything), I said good-bye and I went. Straight to Uunu."

"You just like looking for trouble."

"Yes, but at the beginning I thought I was going to have my desire thwarted and I even thought Rosdolleu didn't know what he was talking about."

"Who was that, your friend from Karperp?"

"Uh-huh. He's president of an institution, a combination ministry and chamber of commerce, and I suspected there might be a question of competition, because I assure you, Uunu was a jewel."

"Later you discovered it was not."

"It was still a jewel, in spite of everything. They acted like gentlemen, they facilitated everything, they found me a cool, sheltered spot where I could leave the clunker open so the wood would be ventilated without having to use the air conditioners, marvelous. They recommended a hotel neither very far away nor right downtown, and when they learned I was a merchant they got me an interview with a boss, Dravato dra Iratoni, who from the name seemed Japanese but wasn't and who called me at the hotel and invited me to dine at his house that same evening. The hotel was gorgeous, comfortable, not very big, with rooms full of light and color and bathrooms with every possible treat."

"Hey, couldn't I go summer on Uunu?"

"I don't advise it."

He waved to someone who was leaving and smoked for a while without saying anything. Would there be coffee on Uunu?

"Was there coffee on Uunu?"

"Yes, there was. Well, relatively speaking."

"Relatively, how? There was or there wasn't."

"There was and there wasn't, you'll see. What was I telling you?"

"That the hotel was splendid and that same night you were going to eat with the Japanese fellow."

"Oh, yes. He had a house to make you laugh at Frank Lloyd Wright. The living room went into the woods, or rather, the woods came into the living room, and the dining room was suspended over the lake. On entering, I thought I would like to live there. Of course, after a short time I would have gotten bored, but for a few weeks, it wouldn't be bad. And he had three delicious daughters and a nice son-in-law, also a merchant like him, and a great big, smiling wife, and he wasn't so big but he was smiling. I had a very good time."

"With which of the three daughters did you go to bed?"

"With none of them. What do you have in your gourd, anyway?"

"Same thing as everyone. And besides, I know you."

"This time, you're way off the mark. Although I confess it was not my virtue but the circumstances that obliged me to chastity. We ate a very tender, very spicy meat, with a kind of sweet potato purée and a flatbread made of different grains, and we drank wine. Afterwards dessert was served and that's where everything started."

"In the dessert?"

"With dessert. I have to tell you that the dishes were display-quality. The owner of the house may not have been Japanese but the plates and the glasses and the jars looked like the very finest Japanese porcelain, in a pale yellow color with a brown border. The dessert arrived served in wooden bowls the same color as the border on the plates, with a wooden spoon. I ate it with relish because it was delicious. I don't know what it was: some fruits like loquats but without pits, a little sour, served in what looked like water but was very sweet, like syrup."

"Big deal. I make better desserts."

"I don't disagree."

That, from Trafalgar, is high praise.

"But this had a very special flavor, and when I finished the fruit I ate the syrup with the spoon. I passed the spoon over the polished wood and as the level of the liquid dropped I felt something very strange."

"An evil spell," I said.

He ignored me.

"I felt, gently at first and then like a kick in the stomach, I felt as if I had made that gesture before, that at some time I had scraped with a wooden spoon the polished bottom of a wooden bowl and that."

"But listen, that happens to all of us."

"Don't I know it," said Trafalgar, and he let Marcos remove the empty cup and leave another, full one, "with all the places I've been to and everything I've done. Generally it isn't true, you never before did what you think you're remembering. A few, very few times it's true, and if you don't remember at the moment, you remember later. But this was much more intense, so much so that I thought I was going to lose my composure. I didn't hear what people were talking about, I didn't see the table, or the faces, or the windows that opened onto the lake. It wasn't me, it wasn't my memory, it was my whole body that remembered the dish and the gesture and, looking at the wood, I recognized even the grain at the bottom," he took out a pencil and drew the lines for me on the back of a card he fished out of his pocket. "See? And here they curved toward the bottom and then rising along the edge they became very, very fine and disappeared."

I stood the card against the water glass. "And then what happened?"

"Nothing. I pulled myself together as best I could and kept talking. We drank liqueurs and coffee, yes, because there was coffee, and we smoked and listened to music and it was after midnight when dra Iratoni's son-in-law drove me back to the hotel. When I was alone in the room, I remembered the thing with the wooden bowl and started to go over it like crazy because I was sure, I knew, sometime, somewhere I had eaten from that bowl. It was no use. I took off my clothes, I bathed, I lay down and I slept. No," he said when I opened my mouth, "I did not dream about the bowl or about the daughters of dra Iratoni. I slept like a log until midday. I woke up hungry. But my hunger went away as soon as I sat up in bed. Speaking of which, don't you want to eat a sandwich or something?"

"No. Go on."

"My hunger and my sleepiness and everything went away, because I was not in the same room in which I had gone to bed. This one was smaller, comfortable but not as cheerful, it was not on the second floor but rather on the tenth or thereabouts, it didn't overlook a park but rather another tall building, and the sunlight didn't come in anywhere. Nor was the bathroom as luxurious as the one in the other hotel, which is to say, I thought I was in another hotel, but."

I wanted to ask him what that meant, but I know when Trafalgar can be interrupted and when he can't.

"It also had its comforts. I didn't stop to bathe or shave. I washed, I went back to the room, and when I was going to the door the horrible idea occurred to me that I had been kidnapped and the door would be locked. It was locked, but the key was on the inside. I turned it with some apprehension and opened the door. It was a hotel, no question. There was a corridor and numbered doors on both sides. Mine was 1247. I looked for the elevator, found it, went down. Twelve floors. The lobby was smaller than the other, cheaper, as if they had wanted to take the fullest advantage of the space."

Here he paused and drank coffee and smoked and I didn't know whether to say something that had occurred to me or not say it, so I kept quiet.

"There was a hoity-toity concierge who asked me, 'Sir?' 'Listen,' I said to him, a little angry now, 'I took a room yesterday in the Hotel Continental; can you tell me where the hell I am now?' 'In the Hotel Continental, sir,' he answered. I was speechless. 'It can't be,' I shouted. 'The room is different and all this, too.' The concierge was unruffled. 'What day did the gentleman arrive?' he asked. I told him the date, day, month, year, and added the hour. 'Ah, that explains everything,' he said. 'How does it explain everything?' I wanted to give him a good wallop while he looked over some papers. 'Room 132 does not exist, sir, at least not at this moment, because the floor has been dedicated to the accounts department and various offices.' And he went to attend to two guys who had just arrived. I thought seriously about jumping over the counter and bashing his face in, but in the first place that wasn't going to accomplish anything and in the second place, what did he mean by saying *at that moment at least* room 132, which was the one I had occupied the day before, didn't exist?"

I decided to drink another coffee and I called Marcos but when he came over I asked if he could make me an orange juice and he said yes.

"Then I went back to room 1247 and inspected my luggage. Everything was in order; it seemed to me that everything was in order. My belly reminded me that it was after midday and I had eaten nothing, so I postponed the problem, went down, went into the restaurant, and ordered the first thing I saw on the menu. And then I remembered the wooden bowl. Once again I felt an urgent physical sensation but I started eating a rather bland stewed fish that they brought me and I thought the best thing would be to go to dra Iratoni's and ask him about what had happened to me. I finished eating, I didn't order dessert, I had coffee, and I went out to the street and froze stiff as a statue. It was another city. It looked like New York. And the day before it had resembled Welwyn. Worse: the cars were different and the people dressed differently. Before I started to get scared at the possibility of not finding dra Iratoni, which was about to happen, I called a taxi that was passing, I climbed in and I told the driver, Paseo de las Agujas 225, and I bet you don't know what I found."

"Look, you could have found anything: a crocodile in the bathtub, or that Paseo de las Agujas didn't exist, or that the driver was Count Dracula, what do I know?"

"The one who didn't exist was the driver."

Marcos brought me an orange juice the way I like it, not strained, without ice, and with very little sugar.

"Trafalgar," I said, "sometimes you depress me. Couldn't you go to Capilla del Monte or Bariloche like everyone else and afterward come tell me that it rained for three days and you lost in the casino and you ran into five guys from Rosario?"

"There are trips on which nothing happens, I assure you. Everything goes well, nothing strange happens, and people do and say what one expects. You don't think I'm going to bring you to the Burgundy to tell you a silly thing like that, I imagine."

"It would be very reassuring," I said. "A while ago, I thought you were a quiet fellow, and you are. But you are not reassuring. At least not when you let fly with things like that. Go on, continue with the phantom taxi driver."

"It was an automatic taxi, driven from a distance, or maybe a robot, I don't know. It didn't start, instead it informed me over a loudspeaker next to the odometer that the old Paseo de las Agujas was impassable for vehicles. I told it to take me as close as possible to the place. Only then did it start. It crossed the city, which was still a twin of New York and not of Welwyn, and stopped in the middle of the country. I tried to get out but the door was stuck. I paid, which is to say I put the money in a collection box, and then the door opened and I got out. It was a park, not very well tended, that extended to the shore of the lake. No woods. I walked along a little path full of stones and weeds as far as the place where I remembered dra Iratoni's house was."

"Which was no longer there," I said.

"No, it wasn't there and I had already begun to suspect that."

"Tell me, hadn't you slept for a couple of centuries like Rip van Winkle?"

"I thought that, too. It would have been an uncomfortable solution but, in the end, reassuring, as you say. I returned to the city on foot. When I arrived, it was almost night. In the suburbs, I took another taxi, also automatic, and I had it take me to the port and I looked for the clunker. And would you believe that I don't know if I found it or no? In the place where it should have been there was a mountain of scrap metal," he made the face Buonarroti would have made, or that I imagine Buonarroti would have made had he seen the Pietá smashed with hammers, "and it could have been in that heap. Sometimes it seemed to me it was, sometimes no. I was so depressed, I didn't even know what to do. Meaning, I knew what I had to do but I didn't know how: I had to find someone who would explain to me what had happened, but I also remembered how little importance the concierge had given to the part of my problem that he knew about—and that irritated me, yet at the same time suggested that everything was probably going to work out easily. I went to the bar in the port, I ate a few sandwiches that tasted like cardboard, I drank some very bad coffee and I pumped up my bad mood until it was pretty late at night. When I left the bar, instead of going to the taxi stand, I headed for the road and I started to walk feeling very sorry for myself. Around then it seemed to me the sun was rising, the sky turned an ugly gray and I had a sensation of unreality and even insecurity, as if I were about to lose my balance, but I didn't pay any attention and I kept walking. It got dark again. I got tired. I sat down on the shoulder, I walked a couple of kilometers or maybe more. I didn't pass a soul and that began to seem strange to me because I had seen earlier that it was a very busy road. When the sun came out for real, I saw the city far off and I had the hope that it had again become Welwyn. My fatigue passed and I picked up my pace. I saw the remains of a burnt truck on the side of the road that, although it had been smooth and new the day before, was quite damaged, full of cracks and potholes. I approached the city. Which, of course, was not Welwyn. Nor was it New York. It was a bombed-out city."

"I know what was happening."

"Not for nothing do you like Philip Dick. I'll tell you, I do, too. But reading a novel or listening when someone tells you the story is one thing, and being thrust into the situation is quite another. I was in no mood that morning to be satisfied with explanations."

The Burgundy was very busy. Almost as if I, no, not I, almost as if Philip Dick had made it fashionable, but Marcos didn't forget about Trafalgar. I stuck to the orange juice.

"I started to see bunkers, trenches, the remains of more trucks and of tanks, too. And bodies. The country was burnt and not a tree remained and there were pieces of walls or some bit of tamped earth where perhaps there had been houses at some time. Someone called out from beyond the shoulder. I turned around and saw a tall, thin guy who was desperately making signs at me. 'Careful! Duck!' he yelled and he threw himself to the ground. I didn't have time. Two military trucks appeared, braked beside me, and five armed soldiers got down and started to kick me around."

"I retract that about wanting to spend the summer on Uunu," I said.

"Many screwy things have happened to me," said Trafalgar; I agreed silently, "but nothing like being knocked down with rifle butts at the side of a road after a sleepless night by some guys in scarlet uniforms appearing from who knows where and without you knowing why or having time to react and defend yourself."

"Scarlet uniforms? What an anachronism."

"The machine guns and bazookas they carried were no anachronism, I can assure you."

69

"Then the question of defending yourself was purely rhetorical."

"Well, yes. First they beat me to a pulp and then they asked who I was. I grabbed my documents but they stopped me short and the one giving the orders called over a soldier who searched me. They looked at everything, passport, identity card, even my driver's license, and they halfway smiled and the head honcho said from up in the truck that they should execute me right then."

"It must be the eighteenth time you escape execution."

"According to my calculations, the third. Once on Veroboar, once on OlogämyiDäa, once on Uunu. I was saved because someone started shooting. And this time I threw myself to the ground and remained, as they say, in critical condition. The tall, thin guy who had yelled to me was coming at the soldiers leading a troop of savages. The soldiers entrenched themselves behind the trucks and started firing, too, and me in the middle. The savages came closer: they were dropping like flies, but they came closer. There were many more of them than of the redcoats and they finally beat them. They killed almost all of them and were left with a lieutenant and two sergeants, wounded but alive. And they lifted me up off the ground and took me with them."

"I'm starting to wonder: from soldiers to savages, I'm not sure where you were going to be better off."

"They looked like savages because they were so grubby and unshaven, but they weren't. They kicked the dead off the road, they took away their weapons, tied up the prisoners—not me—we climbed into the truck and took off jolting like lunatics across the countryside, on the point of overturning every ten meters. We arrived in one piece, I don't know how, at an almost-town or ex-town, and we stopped at a nearly ruined house. One of the sergeants died on the way. The lieutenant was badly wounded but he endured and the other sergeant was more or less all right. They put them in a cellar. To me they gave a foul stew to eat, but if it had been caviar I wouldn't have put it away with more enthusiasm and the tall, thin one who was called ser Dividis sat down with me to ask me as well, but more gently, who I was. I told him. He smiled a little, like the concierge, only I didn't want to hit this guy, and he told me, of course, these things could happen and not to worry, how about that? And that unfortunately they didn't have rhythm charts to inform me with certainty. I didn't know what the rhythm charts were but I wanted a cup of coffee and I asked if there was any. Other guys who were walking around, like they were keeping watch or out of curiosity, burst out laughing, and one who must be my soul mate sighed and closed his eyes. No, ser Dividis told me, it was a long time since there had been coffee. I took out my cigarettes and when I saw their startled, envious faces, I shared them around. They threw themselves on them like castaways: they left me only one, which I smoked while the thin guy explained, not my own case—unfortunately—but the general situation. For my case, there wasn't time."

He sipped coffee very slowly, contrary to his custom.

"They were maquisards, guerrillas, although they melodramatically called themselves Lords of Peace—I don't want to think what the lords of war would be like—and their leaders took the title *ser*. They fought, as best they could, against the Captains. The Captains were a military caste that governed the world after its fashion. Moreover, nothing original. The Lords had been very hopeful lately because the Captains were dividing into groups that fought among themselves, nothing original there, either. Each faction of the Captains had an army with uniforms of a different color. The Reds had just defeated the Yellows and were patrolling the zone killing fugitives and, in passing, Lords. 'Who's winning?' I asked. They had no idea. They were confident of bleeding them dry because the Captains were weakened by fighting each other for absolute power with that tendency people thrown about by death have to believe that absolute power is going to save them from something. And they attacked them using the old technique of appearing where the others least expected them. In addition, and in spite of the fact that the Captains paid well and punished better, there were many desertions and herds of soldiers crossed over to the ranks of the Lords. But I, who know a little history, was not so optimistic. They didn't know anything for certain: there were no newspapers or radios or any kind of communications and land, water, and air transport were in the hands of the Captains, although they stole what they could. They would send spies or messengers to other zones and sometimes men arrived from far away with news that was no longer worth anything. Ser Dividis had been born when the dictatorship of the Captains began to grow powerful and he remembered a little, not a lot, of a world without war. He recounted atrocities, he got worked up, and after a speech that I think was not directed to me or to his men but rather to himself, he asked me what side I was on. I told him on their side, of course, was I going to start arguing?" He thought about it. "Besides, if I had to choose, I would have been with them. I sympathize with lost causes. Which tend to be those that win in the long run and come to power, they become strong, another lost cause appears and everything starts all over again. I was starting to ask ser Dividis why on Uunu I encountered a different world every day when the fight started up again. It was the Reds."

He finished his coffee and pushed the cup away and put his arms on the table, with the cigarette between his joined hands.

"I'm not going to tell you about the battle. One can't. When you have experienced one, the description, the memory, everything you can say, everything you read in the newspaper or saw in the cinema, doesn't go beyond a kindergarten scene. This time they won, the Reds. I had a shotgun someone had put in my hands and I shot out of a window. That lasted quite a while, not as long as it seemed to me at the time, but a while. The Reds had us surrounded and they got closer all the time. I sympathize with lost causes, but I'm not stupid. When I saw the situation was getting ugly, I turned around to see if I could escape somehow, carrying the shotgun and the few bullets I had left. Ser Dividis was doing the same. He made signs to those of us who remained, they pushed aside a table, they raised the floor and we ran away through a subterranean tunnel that came out in the forest. Unfortunately, the Reds were waiting for us in the forest: evidently if the Lords had infiltrators in the armies, the others also had theirs among the Lords' men. They took down almost everyone, including ser Dividis, and I was sorry because he seemed like a good guy; a nutcase, but a good guy. Four of us managed to escape by some miracle into the trees. At last they left us in peace. The other three said that in a half day's march we could reach Irbali so long as there weren't more soldiers on the road, as was very probable: they were crazy, too. I suppose Irbali must be another city, but I said no, I was staying there."

"Doesn't sound very prudent to me."

"The whole world was at war, what did it matter where one was? And I wanted to be close to the port, if it existed, so they left and I remained alone in a forest, with a shotgun in my hand, a dozen bullets, and war all around."

"Yes, of course, the best thing was for you to keep quiet and wait."

"Which I did. Until that moment they hadn't let me decide. But when they left and I could start thinking after a second of panic, I saw that it was best. I didn't know what was going to happen that next day on Uunu, but why lose hope? I climbed a tree, I placed the shotgun in a hollow branch, I arranged myself as best I could in a fork and I waited. When night fell, I climbed down, I grabbed the shotgun and started walking in the direction of the city. I came very close, much sooner than I had imagined: something was burning there which didn't surprise me. I decided to wait for dawn. According to my calculations, if each day I had found a different world, there was no reason the next should be an exception. We would see what happened. Granted, I hoped—or rather, desperately desired—that some day I would return to the world of dra Iratoni and I would be able to leave with my wood. I made the firm resolve, which I did not carry out, to return to Karperp, apologize to Rosdolleu for having thought he was lying to me, and then knock him out with a sucker punch for not having explained to me what was happening and just going on with his elegant evasions. I hid myself as I was able among the plants a good ways off the road, I put the shotgun to one side, I lay down, and I slept."

"'In a bed of silk and feathers / I put my mother and my dreams to sleep.'"

"As if it had been a bed of silk and feathers. I had passed a night without sleeping and a day as an unknown soldier. That was enough: I needed a rest."

"I don't want to rush you, but understand me: I am dying to know what you found the next day."

"The wooden bowl," said Trafalgar.

I had forgotten about the bowl and wasn't expecting it. "The bowl?"

"Yes. Or, at least, a bowl. I woke up and the first thing I saw was that the shotgun had disappeared and it occurred to me that the Yellows or the Reds or the Purples were going to shoot me. The second thing was that I was hungry, incredibly hungry. Also, my unshaved beard made my face itch and my clothes were a mess and I was fed up, understand, fed up."

"Don't get mad," said Marcos, arriving with more coffee and more orange juice. "That won't get you anywhere."

"True," said Trafalgar. "One time I got mad on Indaburd V with the president of the corporation of veltra manufacturers and I lost a fantastic sale."

"See?" said Marcos and he went away very satisfied.

"What's that about veltra?" I said.

"If instead of glass you had veltra in the windows of your house, you wouldn't need heating or air-conditioning, or bars or blinds or curtains."

"I like curtains: they're warm and decorative," I said, and I remembered Uunu. "How was it that you found the bowl that day on Uunu?"

"And also, the president of the corporation of veltra manufacturers was an old idiot."

"Trafalgar, I'm going to kill you."

"You, too?"

And he smiled. So I left him in peace while he drank the coffee that in Rosario, luckily, is not relative.

"All I wanted when it got light," said Trafalgar, "and I saw that it was a horrible morning, cold and gray, was to eat. That the Reds or the Greens might shoot me, fine. I imagined the succulent last feasts of the condemned, with coffee, cigars, and cognac, and my guts twisted with indignation. So I walked toward the city determined that they should kill me, although I imagined, and I liked that but I didn't like it, that the world would be a different one and possibly the Captains would not exist. I required very little, when I reached the city, to recognize that the Captains did not yet exist. Nor was there coffee."

Just in case, he drank the one he had in front of him.

"It was no longer New York nor the bombed-out city but, lamentably, it wasn't Welwyn either. It was a group of huts of coarse brick, possibly dried in the sun, without mortar, with thatch roofs and curtains of branches in the doorways and without windows. There were corrals for the animals and fire pits in a clear central area. They received me well: with great curiosity and a lot of chatter, but well. Men and women had leather loincloths and the kids ran around naked, in that cold. I, of course, fell like a bombshell, although they didn't know what bombs were."

"The war had ended and the world was left like that?"

"The war hadn't started yet. It was centuries before the Captains' war, are you getting this?"

"Damn, of course I get it," I said, "but why didn't anybody warn you?"

"That was more an error on my part than on theirs. But, as I said, they received me well. They approached me with curiosity but without suspicion, they touched me and sniffed at me, chatting and laughing. They were the perfect good savages: if brother Jean Jacques were to see them, he'd tear right up with emotion. I didn't understand what they were saying, and they didn't understand me. But as Raúl says, there are three gestures that work anywhere. They took me to one of the huts and they gave me something to eat. Leaving out the food at dra Iratoni's, it was the best I ate on Uunu. Roast meat and grains cooked with little pieces of fat that were practically cracklings and some green, very juicy fruits. Coffee, of course, out of the question. I regretted having given the cigarettes to ser Dividis' men at the moment when out of habit I put my hand in my pocket, and there was the pack, barely started. I don't know how many I had in the ruined house of the Lords of Peace, but probably nine or ten. And I remembered that on returning that night, the first one, from dra Iratoni's, I had put a full pack and another, just opened, in another pocket of the jacket and the next day, in the new hotel, I had dressed in that suit, which I was still wearing. I had smoked, it's true, in New York and with the Lords, but I looked in a pocket and found the full pack, too, just as predicted. I smoked, something that really got their attention. I was surrounded by kids, by fairly young men and women, who suddenly stepped aside to allow a stooped old man to approach. The old man was completely covered in skins and he had, I suppose as an emblem of authority, rough-made boots also of leather. He came and sat in front of me and began to speak with the alphabet of the mute. He didn't ask me who I was, which is a complicated question to ask with gestures, but he asked where I had come from. I told him the sky and it seemed very good to him. I thanked him for the food and the hospitality and I told him I was pleased. He thanked me for my gratitude and we were already great friends. I also told him I was tired and then, as I saw that the men had long hair but not beards, I told him I wanted to shave. What for? You can imagine they didn't bring me a Phillips or even a Techmatic. They talked a little and a matron appeared bringing some stones that were shiny from so much use. I backed away, plenty scared, but it was too late." He grew pensive. "I have been shaved in many parts of this world and of others. In London, for example, and in Venice and in Hong Kong; and also on Oen, on Enntenitre IV, on Niugsa and in the City of the Beings—some day I'll have to tell you what that is. But no one ever shaved me so well, so softly or so close, so thoroughly, so maternally as that fat matron dressed in a loincloth, adorned with necklaces and bracelets made from the teeth of some animal, almost toothless, dying of laughter and with two stones as her only equipment. The others were also laughing because I was terrified she would cut my jugular or my nose or both of them, but by the time I finished explaining with signs that I had changed my mind and I no longer wanted to be shaved, I could have been dead and buried. I made the fat woman understand that the mustache, no, and that also surprised her and they laughed at that, too. She sharpened the small stone against the other, moistened my face with something that seemed like broth, and began. When she was halfway through, I was already calmer and when she finished, I grabbed her by both hands and I shook them up and down and I laughed, I let her go and I gave her a pat on the back and everyone was happy. You won't believe me, but it was the most peaceful day I spent on Uunu. I ate, I slept, they took me around and I even got close to the place where the port should have been."

"Which wasn't there, nor the Japanese fellow's house nor anything."

"Nothing. Except the lake, which perhaps was bigger. And the woods, which was practically a forest. It was a fabulous day. You can't say it was perfect because we had a visitor."

"I would almost bet money it was a tyrannosaurus."

"You just missed by a little. A saber-toothed tiger, so long as saber-toothed tigers were as I imagine them. It seems it had been roaming around eating people and animals, and in the early evening a party went out—as they had been doing for a good while, the old man explained in a conversation that gave us both quite a bit of trouble—they found it and they chased it into a trap they had prepared. But the fellow was well versed in traps and got loose. It didn't attack, because it was well fed, but, surrounded on all sides, it escaped toward the village. It reached the edge of the land occupied by the huts and there was a big clamor and people scattered in all directions and then the men of the village that had been chasing it appeared and they killed it with lances and axe blows. It was a slaughter. All were left wounded and one dead. But with a sophistication unlooked for in noble savages, first came the celebration and afterward the grief. There was a feast with song and dance which the wounded and the dead attended as guests of honor. They skinned the tiger and we ate the meat: the main course was the entrails marinated in something like vinegar, and the heart, chopped up very fine, of which we each ate a piece."

"Eating the vanquished enemy," I said. "What would brother Jean Jacques think of that?"

"Who knows? The tiger was tough, imagine, newly dead meat of a cornered animal accustomed to running and climbing. It wasn't exactly pheasant, or even close. Dark, fibrous meat, but not at all bland and without a bit of fat. Did I tell you they served the chopped heart in a wooden bowl?"

"No, you didn't tell me. Was it the same bowl from which you'd eaten the seedless loquats at dra Iratoni's?"

77

"No, it wasn't the same."

"But then where are we?"

"When I saw the bowl arrive I felt good, as if I no longer had any worries—and did I ever have them. It was like meeting an old, long-lost friend and I almost believed everything was solved, that if this was what I had remembered that night, all the rest of it was no longer important. Nonsense, of course, but I was celebrating the death of the tiger and eating its entrails and drinking the fermented juice of something and you know with all that, a certain irresponsibility gets into one. Especially after having seen how a saber-toothed tiger dies. As the bowl was full and I served myself my little bit but there was still a lot left, I watched as it passed from hand to hand until it was empty. They set it down and I stood up to get it. I cleaned it."

"With a wooden spoon to complete the reminiscence."

"Wooden spoons in the stone age, come on."

"Well, yes," I said, "spoons are almost as old as knives."

"Let's not exaggerate," said Trafalgar.

"Neolithic," I insisted, "in the Neolithic there were already spoons."

"Could be. But not on Uunu of Neyiomdav. I cleaned it with my fingers. It wasn't the same. It looked a lot like it, that's true."

"Of course it looked like it. All wooden bowls look like each other. You can't make great modifications with something so simple."

"Yes, but it wasn't the same. It was made of different wood, it was deeper, it didn't have the same grain. And in addition, I felt nothing: it wasn't the same, I tell you."

"I believe you. What I want to know, and right away, is if you ever found that other bowl."

"I found it," he said, "but not there. I kept the bowl in my hand and I even asked the old man if I might have it as a gift and he gave it to me with great courtesy. I lost it afterwards, of course, for the same reason I had lost the shotgun and recovered the cigarettes and the documents. And, speaking of which, I smoked the last one before lying down to sleep."

"I am terrified," I said. "What did you find the next day?"

"Cheer up, here comes the best part."

What came was more coffee in the hand of Marcos. Trafalgar's trips don't interest Marcos. I suspect he doesn't believe him. And he's interested in other things: in the Burgundy, his kids, the first grandchild (due in the next three months), his wife, Clarisa, who was beauty queen in 1941 in Casilda, race horses and, something in common with Trafalgar, tango.

"I woke up in the Hotel Continental," Trafalgar said with his nose deep in his cup.

"Which one?"

"The first. Dirty, with my suit immaculate, well shaven and without the bowl or the shotgun but with my documents and a pack and a half of cigarettes in my jacket pockets. I got up, I looked out the window, and I was in the city that resembled Welwyn and my room was number 132 on the second floor and it overlooked a park. I ran my hand over my face and I felt an immense tenderness toward the fat woman. I bathed, I put on another suit and went down to have breakfast. Liters of coffee."

"I don't doubt it."

"And some crunchy fritters and more coffee and cigarettes. Afterward, I grabbed a phone and called dra Iratoni; I was scared, you wouldn't believe, but I called. Only when I heard his voice did I know for sure that I was back on the Uunu to which I'd arrived. He invited me again to dine at his house and I said no thank you, I wanted to see him that very morning. Then he gave me the address of a club or businessmen's circle and told me he'd meet me there. I took a taxi—with a driver—I went to the port, inspected the clunker and the wood and found everything was fine, I took another taxi and I went to the club. There I had to endure almost an hour of introductions and conversations with other merchants who were with dra Iratoni, until I managed to drag him to a little room and buttonhole him myself."

"Last chapter," I said, "and thank goodness, because it's getting late."

"Stay and eat downtown," said Trafalgar.

"I can't. Besides, if I stay you're going to extend the story until we finish our dessert, whereas this way you have no alternative but to tell me everything now. And if they were to serve us dessert in wooden bowls, I'd have an attack. So go on."

"I told dra Iratoni everything," he said, "and he listened to me with great formality, like the concierge, like ser Dividis, but, like them, he wasn't the least bit worried. He did say, at least, that he was sorry not to have said anything, but that he had assumed I was informed because if I had said on Karperp that I was going to Uunu, they would have already warned me. When I told him no, on Karperp they had insinuated something and had told me it wasn't a good idea to go and for that very reason I had come, he was enormously surprised. He stood there with his mouth open and his jaw dropping. How? If a guy wants to go somewhere, why not say so? And if they tell him he shouldn't go, why would he go? Or why not insist and ask for explanations and afterward decide whether to go or not? A Neyiomdaviano does not understand our give and take."

"They must be great people."

"I assure you, they are. A little unsettling. But I maintain that yes, they're terrific. They say what they think, or they give you a subtle invitation, which to me sounded like reluctance, for you to say what you think, and they say what they are going to do and they do what they have said they are going to do. It's not as easy as it seems."

"Must not be much room for neurosis there."

"You know there's always room for neurosis, everywhere. But it seems to me we give it more consideration than the Neyiomdavianos. I made dra Iratoni understand some of this and then he explained to me what happens on Uunu and I am going to try to explain it to you but I don't know if I'll be able to."

He finished his coffee and took a breath as if for a pole vault.

"Time is not successive," he said. "It is concrete, constant, simultaneous, and not uniform."

Then I was the one who took a breath.

"God, for instance," said Trafalgar, "perceives it that way, and every religion allows that. And on Uunu it's perceptible that way for everyone, although with a lesser immediacy, due to a quirk of its placement in space. Space which, of course, could not exist without its coexistant, time."

"We're not getting anywhere this way," I said. "Give me the concrete examples because I don't read Einstein or Langevin or Mulnö."

"Imagine time," said Trafalgar, "as an infinite and eternal—it's the same thing—bar of a material that has different degrees of consistency both in its duration and in its length. With me?"

"Got it."

"Now, once a day, or rather once a night, Uunu experiences a chrono-synclastic infundibulum."

"Oh, no," I protested. "That's from Vonnegut."

"Yes. And dra Iratoni didn't say it like that but in another way, much more descriptive but also more complicated, so much so that I don't remember it well. But you know the chrono-synclastic infundibulum. When it occurs, it covers and envelops all of Uunu and then the parts of that temporal bar that at that moment have greatest consistency, surface—I can't think of another way to say it—and so if today is today, tomorrow can be a hundred years from now or ten thousand five hundred years ago."

"I understand now," I said. "I think so, at least. But the people of each era, don't they find themselves thrown from one to another and have to live a different moment of their history every day? Why did you not meet dra Iratoni the next day even though his house didn't exist, or how come the concierge from the first Hotel Continental wasn't in the second one?"

"No, no. Each continues with their life in the era they were born in and in which they live, thanks to their adaptation to the environment. A lousy environment, I'll agree with you, but not worse than others. Eras don't mix, one never invades another. They coexist. They are simultaneous. If you're born on Uunu, you keep living your life day by day, very happy, unaffected and you know that at the same time other things are happening in other eras. With a little effort of the syncretic awareness of time—I don't know what it is, but dra Iratoni takes it for granted that all of us have it—you can perceive on any given day of your life, the era which on that precise day has the greater consistency since the prior chrono-synclastic infundibulum. Something no one on Uunu bothers to do, or almost no one. They're prevented by the very fact that all eras are there, as they say, within reach. Historians or philosophers or sociologists do it—or have done it—to demonstrate something, always discreetly and without bothering anyone or getting involved. Or a few crackpots or maniacs, which are almost nonexistent on Uunu so there aren't problems on that side. I don't know if the sensitivity of the Neyiomdavianos of Uunu doesn't come from knowing the consistency of time and knowing they could avail themselves of it if they wished."

"But wait," I said, "then you were bouncing here and there, from the future to the Captains to the Neolithic, because you were a foreigner and weren't adapted?"

"I was born in Rosario, not on Uunu. I don't have a syncretic awareness of time or if I have it, it's atrophied. And to top it off, I have the eagerness, the anguish of time. In me, time isn't something natural, a part of me, it's almost a saddlesore. In me and in all of us. I got to Uunu and I was defenseless for that reason—floating, let's say. And when the chrono-synclastic infundibulum came along, there I went to the most consistent part of that eternal and infinite temporal unity."

"I don't want to think about the matter too much. It's very simple and very complicated."

"Very. And very unpleasant. Now notice that on the first night, when I went to bed in room 132 of the Hotel Continental and dra Iratoni and his family went to sleep in their house, for me, who am not an adapted native, there followed the morning of many years later and I woke up in a Hotel Continental that was going to exist, in a changed city, with robot taxis and skyscrapers. The next day, hundreds of years later, under the paranoid tyranny of the Captains, and the next, in the Stone Age. But the next, when I once again woke up in room 132, dra Iratoni and his family woke up on the morning after the night when I had been having dinner at their house."

"But how? And those three days in which you were going from one side to the other of Uunu's history?"

"For them, they didn't exist or, better put, they didn't elapse, because as far as existing, they always exist. For them the chrono-synclastic infundibulum of my first night on Uunu was an everyday event that their syncretic awareness of time can ignore. I was snatched away to a hundred or two hundred years later and there another chrono-synclastic infundibulum carried me various centuries later when there was another that carried me to thousands of years before and so on until I was returned to the world of dra Iratoni, luckily. He explained to me, furthermore, that sooner or later that was going to happen, and he showed me the rhythm charts that are something like logarithm tables but thicker than the Tokyo telephone book and that predict toward where and when the most consistent parts of time are moving every night."

"I was mistaken," I said. "It's more complicated than I thought. But tell me—so they know both what has happened and what is going to happen?"

"Of course. From the point of view of knowledge, it's very useful. And if you need something that has not been discovered, you get into a syncretic temporal trance or whatever it is and you find out, because the rhythm charts tell you when the time in which you believe whatever it is will be already known will be most consistent. Now, from the personal point of view, with the good sense and the calm they have about everything, it doesn't occur to anyone to try to spy into the future to see when or how they're going to die or anything like that. I think that would be frowned upon, I don't mean as criminal but definitely as something that would discredit one."

"No, what I mean is, if they know the dictatorship of the Captains, which from what I see looks pretty bad, is going to come along some day, why don't they do something to change things now so it doesn't happen?"

"Can you stand another turn of the screw?"

"Well, yes, what do you expect me to do?"

"I told you to imagine time as an infinite and eternal bar of varying consistency, right?"

"Yes."

"Well, it is possible that there are infinite eternal and infinite bars, et cetera."

"Oh, no."

"Think about the arborescent universes."

I said nothing: I thought about the arborescent universes.

"What in reality coexists isn't time, a time, but the infinite variants of time. That's why the Neyiomdavianos of Uunu do nothing to modify the future, because there isn't a future, there isn't anything to modify. Because on one of those bars, those variants, those branches, the Captains don't come to power. In another, the one who comes to power is ser Dividis. In another Welwyn doesn't become New York. In another dra Iratoni doesn't exist, in another he exists but he's a bachelor schoolteacher, in another he exists and he is what he is and as he is but he doesn't have a house stuck out into the woods and the lake that would make Frank Lloyd Wright kill himself from envy if he saw it, in another I never come to Uunu, in another Uunu is uninhabited, in another."

"All right," I said. "Enough."

Marcos came to bring coffee and I asked him for a small one for myself.

"Seriously?" Marcos said. "You don't want another orange juice? Or grapefruit juice?"

"No, seriously, a coffee. I need something stronger than juice."

Marcos laughed and told me he was going to bring me a double whiskey and I said if he did, I would never set foot in the Burgundy again and he laughed a little more.

"Something's missing," I said to Trafalgar. "What happened with the wooden bowl?"

"I'm going to tell you. When dra Iratoni finished, I told him I was leaving that very day and he answered that it seemed the safest course. But he invited me to lunch at his home and I accepted. I had flowers sent to Madame Iratoni and I went and found the whole family and I again had a very good time and dessert was served in a crystal dish and not in wooden bowls. I went to the hotel, I paid, I took out my luggage and I went to the port and readied the clunker.

My friend Iratoni came to say good-bye along with two of those business cronies he had introduced me to that morning, he gave me some bottles of wine from Uunu and I cast off. I sold the wood on Anidir XXII, where they bargain like Bedouins, but, as wood is a luxury item there—as it is going to be here before long—I made them take the bit and pay what I wanted and I left."

"And the bowl?"

"Oh, the bowl. Look, I planned to travel again a week later. But three days after I arrived, I ran into Cirito and Fina at a concert and they invited me to dinner the next day. You know I prefer going to Cirito's when Fina isn't there, but they insisted and I had to say yes. I went, we ate in the garden because it was quite hot, almost like today. Cirito gave himself the treat of doing a barbeque and he served the meat on those boards that come with a channel on the side and rustic utensils. So as not to clash, there were raffia rounds for placemats, and dessert came in wooden bowls. It wasn't loquats without seeds but chocolate cream with meringue on top. And when I scraped, with that rustic, wooden spoon, the bottom of the bowl."

"I know."

"You guessed it. Then, only then, did I understand what dra Iratoni had told me and I guessed much more. I think that not only do all of us, everywhere, have a syncretic awareness of time, but also that everywhere infinite variants of what has happened and what is going to happen and what is happening coexist, and maybe at some points and at some instants they cross and you think you remember something you have never experienced or that you could have experienced or that you could experience and will not experience, or as in my case with the bowl, that you come to experience if there is the almost impossible juncture, I don't want to call it chance, of two crossings in which you are present. It is a memory, because in one or in some variants of time you experienced it or you will experience it, which is the same. And it is not a memory, because most likely in your line of variants it has not happened nor is it ever going to happen."

"Let's go," I said. "Pay and let's go, because I've had enough for today."

And while Marcos went to get the change, Trafalgar put out the next to last cigarette, looked at the card on which he had drawn the grain of the bowl for me, put it back in his pocket and said, "Don't forget that every day is the best day of the year. I don't know who said that, but it's true."

"I can imagine where this advice is leading," I answered.

Marcos brought a pile of bills on a little plate, he left it on the table, waved his hand, and went back behind the bar.

On the street, it was still very hot.

"I'll walk you to the bus stop," Trafalgar said.

The González Family's Fight for a Better World

Excess profits, that's what I'd say. And in every sense of the word, because Edessbuss is an amiable world where everyone finds humor and an occasion for fun in everything. One almost—almost—starts to want to stay there to live, but if one maintains a bit of sense, not easy to do after a week of partying, one realizes that amusing oneself for two weeks or a year or three months is all very well, but to spend one's whole life playing, for one who wasn't born there, must be as boring as toiling thirty years as an office worker on Ortauconquist or on Earth. Yes, costumes, a shipment of costumes, masks, veils, confetti, streamers, and balloons, the works. I have bought and sold many crazy things in all these years, but until then I had never traveled with boxes of masks and perfume-sprayers. I already knew Edessbuss because I buy the clay from them that I sell on Dosirdoo IX where they make the finest porcelains, china, and ceramics in that whole sector, but I had never stayed more than a day or two, enough for the purchase and the loading. Really nice people, always good humored, easy to make friends with. I have a couple of excellent friends there, The Owner of the Cold Winds and The Toughest Tamer of the Pale, Pale Star. Not counting The Duchess of Bisque or The Splendorous Girl, who are two fantastic people. No, no, those are their names, they're not titles or nicknames. At twelve years old, each one chooses their definitive name and as they have imagination and a sense of humor and everything is permitted, the results are terrific. And that's not all. I met the Blue and Glaucous Giant, and Possessed by Women, The Angel

Archangel Ultraangel, The Savage Captainess of the Storm Clouds, The Inventor of a New Color Every Day, The SuperFat Empress— anyway, you would not believe. Of course, what happened that time was there was a problem in Flight Control in the port and they asked me to suspend my departure, if I could, while they planned I don't know what all arrivals, departures, and layovers. I stayed, of course. A week of partying, as I said. Then I learned things had not always been so easy. Edessbuss was an inhospitable world, almost dead. Seriously: it is the only one that revolves around Edess-Pálida, a killer star. It gives off so much energy, it burnt up plants, animals, rivers, and people. For generations and generations, hundreds, thousands of years, the Edessbussianos lived in semi-subterranean hovels, fighting against the heat, the droughts, the plagues, the floods, hunger, until finally, their brains racked to the maximum by so much misfortune, they invented the Roof. No, they call it the Roof but it's a screen, an anti-energy cover that surrounds the whole world. What the theoretical principle is or how they placed it, that I don't know. All of us who go to Edessbuss, and there are a lot of us, the majority to have a good time and a few like me to do business, cross it with no problems, we don't even notice. The energy from Edess-Pálida doesn't pass, or rather it passes up to a certain point: enough to turn Edessbuss into a garden full of lakes and flowers and birds. And then, and it could hardly be otherwise, for the last five hundred years the Edessbussianos have been getting even for everything that those who lived before the Roof had to go through. Everyone laughs, sings, dances, makes love, plays, makes up games and jokes. And I was the victim of one of those jokes. But I bear them no grudge. First because you can't, they're too nice. And two because the result was more than interesting. If I was a sentimental person, and I probably am, I would say it was touching. Yes, I'm getting to that. As I was saying, I stayed a week, in a hotel bungalow on the shores of Lucky Bounce Lake where one had to resign oneself to sleeping fitfully because there was a party every night. Of course, there's no place on Edessbuss where they're not having a party every night, so it didn't matter where I stayed. And nevertheless, they know how to do business, believe me. Between laughter and exaggerations and jokes, but nothing escapes them, it's a pleasure to see. No, I had already delivered the merchandise, the costumes and all that, and they had paid me and very well—hence my comment about excess profits. Of course they weren't giving charity but sweetening me up for the next order and then we'd see, but as I knew it and they knew I knew it, we all took advantage without bitterness, they of the costumes and I of the cash, and devoted ourselves to having a good time. The true art of fun is learned on Edessbuss: no one rolls under the table drunk, no one vomits from eating too much, no one has a heart attack while trying to break records in bed. There aren't fights, no one comes to blows with anyone over a woman because in the end they can have as many as they like. And as the women can have as many men as they like, they're good-humored and they're prettier all the time and a forty-year-old easily gets the better of a twenty-year-old and the seventy-year-olds stroll around with the airs of queens of the world and deign, when they're in the mood, to teach subtleties to the eighteen-year-old guys. But yes, of course they work. And they study and they look through the microscope and they write novels and they pass laws. Like anywhere else. Only the spirit of the thing is different: for them, life is not a tragedy. It was a tragedy, before the Roof. Nor is it a farce; it's a cheerful comedy that always ends well. A judge can let out a guffaw in the middle of a trial if the prosecutor says something funny, and an atomic physicist who is the dean of a college can meticulously prepare a monster joke for his students, and if the oldest kid took dad's car out without permission, the old man falls over laughing and puts half a dozen toads in the boy's bed and hides in the closet to see what happens. I assure you, it's just a matter of getting used to it. The first day, one doesn't know which way to turn. On the second, one starts to laugh. On the third, one imagines playing a joke, or invents one to tell, nothing original yet. And on the fourth, one's a veteran. Go figure what I was after a week. But even so, they made me fall in their trap. That last night, to say good-bye, The Toughest Tamer of the Pale, Pale Star took me to a party at The SuperFat Empress's place—she has a kind of Babylon with hanging gardens but smaller—and they made me fall like a fool. At midnight,

I said I was going to bed, I had an early departure scheduled for the next day. No one tries to convince anyone of anything there and no one contradicts you: courtesy is something else. If one wants to leave, one leaves; if one wants to stay, one stays; and when the host decides the party is over, he says good-bye to everyone and everyone accepts it and no one thinks it's wrong. I said I was leaving and they crowded around to wish me a good night. A really nice little guy, The Crazy Minstrel of the Still Waters, asked where I was headed and I said I was going home after stopping at Dosirdoo IX and Jolldana.

"Too bad," he said, "because Gonzwaledworkamenjkaleidos is very close and it is a fabulous place for business."

The others were in agreement—too much in agreement and too loudly, I thought later, when it was too late. But at that moment I didn't notice, because the name had caught my attention.

"What?" I said. "What is it called?"

"Gonzwaledworkamenjkaleidos," they repeated.

"You can sell anything there," said The Savage Captainess of the Storm Clouds, "and the silver bells they make are the prettiest I've heard."

Silver bells, of course, why not? But the thing tempted me. I asked where it was and the husband of The SuperFat Empress, whose name is Shield of Fire that Roars at Night, went to look for a route guide. They told me they would give me all the details at the port and they asked what I might be carrying to sell. I had the clay, of course, but that was for Dosirdoo IX, and I also had anilines, iron fittings, and plastic pipes. And medicines.

"That's it," yelled The Crazy Minstrel of the Still Waters. "They always need those! Medicines!"

"Vitamins," someone said.

"Tonics!" The SuperFat Empress clapped her hands. "Tonics, tonics, tonics, tonics!"

"Cough syrup, anti-diarrheals, anorectics, neuroleptics, vasodilators, skin ointments, laxatives, antifungals." They hollered out every kind of medication they could think of and they laughed, of course, how could they not laugh?

I managed to pull one of them, The Twelfth Knight of the Order of the Checked Doublet, into a corner and ask him what the probabilities were. He swore by his collection of bamboo cats that on Gonzwaledworkamenjkaleidos I could sell whatever I wanted and above all medicines because they went crazy about medicine and they didn't haggle. All of which, I am sorry to say, was basically true, although in this case the nuances are important. So The Twelfth Knight of the Order of the Checked Doublet's collection of bamboo cats must be sitting pretty in its display cabinet. Yes, the next day I went to that world. I slept well that night in spite of the music and the dancing at the hotel, I composed the route at the port, and I left. The Splendorous Girl came to see me off, in her chief nurse's uniform, along with The SuperFat Empress before she went to the studio; The Toughest Tamer of the Pale, Pale Star, in a hurry because he had a meeting with the directors of the factory; The Crazy Minstrel of the Still Waters, very imposing as a Police corporal; and others that I don't remember. The Twelfth Knight of the Order of the Checked Doublet sent a message because he was on call at the hospital. No, thank you, do serve yourself, I never take sugar. Of course it was close, I arrived almost immediately. It's the fourth of a system of six, the only inhabited one, quite large, and it moves at a normal speed. I started to descend and to signal, looking for a port. No one answered me. And even that didn't alarm me, see what an idiot? I flew low, still looking for a port, and nothing. It seemed strange, yes, but I didn't get suspicious: I was still dazzled by the Edessbussianos' enthusiasm. A little irritated by now, I chose a city, low, not very big but the largest one I found, and I landed in the countryside, as close as I could. When I was getting close to the ground, let's say two hundred, two hundred fifty meters, what do I find? You will never believe it. An aerostat. A balloon, yes sir, it's incredible. A balloon uglier than a fat chick in a bikini, painted gray with darker stripes, as if camouflaged. Hey, these guys are at war, I thought, and I tried to remember if I was carrying coagulants, antibiotics, and disinfectants and if anything else might serve in case of trouble. I don't sell arms, it's the one place I don't compromise. Everything else, from livestock on the hoof to diamonds from Quitiloe. Did you ever see a diamond from Quitiloe? My friend, you don't know what you're missing. The opposite of ours, the smaller they are, the more expensive. You understand why when they pass you one and you have it in your hand. The smallest one I ever saw measured two millimeters by two millimeters and weighed five and a half kilos. There are some that measure a meter in length and weigh hardly anything. If they're longer than a meter they use them as mirrors but mounted on the wall because otherwise they float away. No, why would they be at war? I realized that before I descended and I stopped thinking about coagulants. I passed close to the balloon and I saw it had a wicker basket hanging below it and in the basket were three guys with frightened faces who watched and pointed at me. I waved my hand at them and gave them a big smile but they didn't even answer. Yes, of course. You won't have any more? Well, thank you. I landed in the middle of the countryside, very close to the city. I made fast in lift-off position, a precaution I always take when I arrive at a place for the first time. I packed a temporary bag, put in papers and documents because one never knows where they're going to ask for them, I left the clunker, connected the alarms, and I stopped with my satchel in hand in the middle of a field. All of this took me a good while, but I had done things slowly on purpose to give the people of the city sufficient time to approach. Would you believe, no one appeared? I don't trust that kind of thing. It has happened to me other times, believe me. On Eertament, on Laibonis VI, on Rodalinzes and, unless I'm very much mistaken, on a couple of other worlds as well. Of course, it might not be hostility or even indifference, but rather a norm of good manners, really rather strange for us. On Laibonis VI, for example, where they carefully avoided me for an entire day, it was, incredibly, an expression of interest, deference, and even respect. On the other hand, on Eertament things began that way and ended badly, very badly. So I took a few measures. I don't use weapons: not only do I not sell them, I don't use them. But I have a very useful little device that was given to me years ago on Aqüivanida, where there are more animals than people and some of them are dangerous but it is forbidden to kill them, which recharges on its own, adapts to any metabolism, and causes reversible, temporary devastation, long enough so one can get away. I went to get it, I hung it from my wrist, grabbed my satchel, and started to walk toward the city. Did you ever see *La Kermesse héroïque?* Great movie. I've already told the Cinema Club people that I'll become a member if they promise to show it once a year. Do you remember the first scenes? That's what the city was like. It's called Gonzwaledworkamenjkaleidaaa. Seriously, it seems like one is never going to learn it, but that's the least of it. The buildings were crude, stubby, old, ugly. The streets were not paved and there were little stone bridges to cross the irrigation ditches. The animals walked around loose. There was a plaza with a market, and people were dressed in the most outlandish fashion: some looked made to order for the heroic kermesse, others were like troglodytes with skins and everything, I saw two boys in jeans and T-shirts and there were others who looked like the baby brothers of Louis XV. I stopped a guy who had on a leather apron over his pants and an old-fashioned shirt and asked where there was a hotel. There were no hotels. We've started badly, I said. An inn? There were no inns. A hostel? There were no hostels. A monastery? Yes, you heard me right; trust me, if you ever go to a godforsaken place in which there are no hotels or boarding houses or anything, ask for the monastery. There were no monasteries.

"But then," I say to the guy, "where does a traveler stay?"

"He has to ask permission in some house," he tells me, and he leaves.

I let fly a discreet insult under my breath and kept walking. Around the plaza, no way, too much noise. I turned down one of the streets that opened off the market and walked a block. People looked at me, but they could hardly pretend to ignore me quickly enough. If it hadn't been because I still thought I could sell something, I'd have gone back to the clunker and left. But you always have to be sure you can't do anything before you fold—I know what I'm talking about. Then I see a guy in the doorway of a house that is neither better nor worse than the rest and I go over and I tell him they've informed me there are no hotels and could he give me lodging. Here, please, smoke one of mine; yes, they're black. The fellow looked at me with curiosity, but let's call it

93

a friendly curiosity, and I think he even started to smile at me. But then he got serious and said he would go ask. He went inside and left me on the street. I used the time to look over the whole block and I didn't see anything new, except a round face in a window of the house next door. The owner of the face looked at me quite openly and, just in case, I did not smile. She was the one who smiled. I didn't have time to return the compliment because my possible host returned and told me no, it wasn't authorized. Like that, no *look I'm really sorry but.* No, he told me no, they didn't authorize it. I told him I was prepared to pay whatever price he asked and he didn't even answer and he went back into the house. Normally, I would not have said something so imprudent, but apart from the fact that I had money to spare, I was determined come hell or high water to get into one of those houses and see how these disagreeable people, who flew in balloons and had neither ports nor hotels, managed things. I took two steps to go try my luck somewhere else and right then the window of the house next door opened and someone said hello. Yes, it was the owner of the round face. Thank goodness, I thought, and I also said hello.

"What did my cousin tell you?" she asked.

"Your cousin?" I said. "That man is your cousin?"

"Of course. We're all cousins on Gonzwaledworkamenjkaleidos."

"Well, how nice," I managed, a little confused.

"What did he tell you?"

"No."

"No, what?"

"That he can't put me up."

She started to laugh. She had perfect teeth and she was quite pretty—granted, not very young—and pleasant. At least she knew how to laugh, not like everyone else there who walked around with funeral faces, and funeral face, I'm telling you, was exactly the right expression.

"Tell me, ma'am," I go and I ask her, "you wouldn't have space to put me up?"

"I do," she said, "and my cousin does, too. He's just a wimp. Wait and I'll open the door for you."

She disappeared from the window and a little while later she opened the door and invited me in. She was between thirty-five and forty years old, not very tall, generous in the body as in the face without being fat. I left the satchel on the ground and introduced myself.

"I am Ribkamatia Gonzwaledworkamenjkaleidos," she told me. That left me cold.

"What? Isn't that the name of this world of yours?"

"Yes," she said, "and we're all called that: we're the Gonzwaledworkamenjkaleidos family."

"Look," I answered, "that's very complicated for me. How would it be if I abbreviate it to González, which is a very common name in my country?"

She laughed and said she had no problem with that, and she showed me the house. From the outside it was as modest, as unattractive, as the rest. But inside, the carnival continued. The floors were black and white tile. There were lace curtains in the windows; the furniture was solid, dark; simple but comfortable. And there was a lot of wood and a lot of white china and copper everywhere and everything was clean and shining. I liked it. But there was no electric light. No, there wasn't. Don't trouble, I'll serve myself. Excellent coffee, this. Yes, of course it surprised me, but I have seen so many strange things. And one learns not to question until the right moment. The house had three bedrooms, hers with an enormous double bed. I hoped the husband would be as friendly and pleasant as she was but I didn't need to worry because she told me shortly that she was a widow and lived alone. She offered me another bedroom, it had a bed that was smaller but it was well furnished, a dresser with a mirror, a bedside table, an armchair, a red rug and also lace curtains at the window that opened onto the back garden. I asked her the price and she named such a ridiculous sum that I was embarrassed. And in addition, she asked if I wanted meat or fish for lunch.

"But, ma'am," I protested, "I thought the price was only for lodging. I planned to eat in a restaurant."

"There are no restaurants," she said.

I should have expected that. Where had those cretins on Edessbuss sent me? A world without hotels and without restaurants, without pavement, without electric light, with sad, terrified people who traveled by balloon, come on. Of course, maybe they needed medicines. And also anilines or plastic pipes, we would see. I didn't say anything and I asked her if I could take a bath. She said of course and indicated a door at the end of the hallway. And she made me her most decided supporter when she added:

"While you bathe, I am going to make you a cup of hot coffee."

"Without sugar or milk, please," I told her as I went into the bath.

What a bath, my goodness. Not because it was luxurious or sophisticated: it rather resembled my maternal grandmother's bath, at the estate in Moreno. It was enormous, with walls and ceiling paneled in strips of polished wood and a white tile floor. The fixtures were also large, very large, of white china, and the bathtub stood on a wooden platform. The faucets were bronze and sparkled like Quitiloe diamonds. There was a window close to the ceiling and white towels with fringes hanging on the hooks. I turned a faucet uncertainly, but soon I had the tub full of hot water and I took the most nostalgic bath of my life. I emerged, a new man, into the corridor that smelled of freshly brewed coffee. I went to the kitchen—the bathroom's twin—and Ribkamatia González protested because she wanted to serve me in the dining room, but I sat down at the white wooden table and drank the coffee, which was fantastic. I asked if she wouldn't join me but she said she didn't drink coffee: women are often funny that way. I took out a cigarette and I must have hesitated a little because she told me it didn't bother her if I smoked; she didn't smoke, no one smoked in public on González, but I was her guest and it didn't bother her. So I smoked and tipped the ashes into a saucer and I talked nonsense, and when I finished the coffee she offered me another, and when I finished the second coffee I started trying to find out what I had to do to sell my merchandise. She didn't know, but she thought it would be difficult. She thought about it a moment and told me I should go speak to the mayor and she explained where I had to go and asked me when I wanted to have lunch. Very agreeable, being attended to in that fashion, but it seemed to me an imposition and as the morning was ending, I said at whatever time she ate, as I was going to be out for an hour, more or less. She made a face that said she didn't really believe me, but she said fine and went to wash the cup. I said good-bye and went out. Cousin González was once again in the doorway and he looked at me as he had earlier but I did not greet him. I went to the plaza, located the building belonging to the municipality or whatever it was, went in and said I wanted to see the mayor. They didn't ask what I wanted or make me wait. Besides, the mayor wasn't doing anything. He was seated in front of an empty table looking sadly out the window. We greeted each other, I said who I was and he said he was Ebvaltar González, well, not González but Gonzwaledworkamenjkaleidos. I explained that I was a merchant and I wanted a permit to sell, and the guy started to stammer and put up objections. Then I pulled the medicines out of my sleeve—so to speak—and told him I had vitamins, tonics, cough syrups. His sadness ended and panic seized him. No, no, not possible, what did I mean, medicines, I was crazy, you couldn't sell that there, it wasn't permitted, good heavens, how could I think of such a thing.

"The Crazy Minstrel of the Still Waters be damned," I said, remembering the scene at the home of The SuperFat Empress when I left and realizing, at last, that it had all been a joke on the part of my friends on Edessbuss; and although I was angry, I almost wanted to laugh.

"What did you say?" asked the mayor.

"Nothing, don't worry, it has nothing to do with you," I answered. "But tell me, why can't one sell medicines here? To protect the local pharmaceutical industry?"

"No, no," he stammered.

"Everyone enjoys good health?"

"No, no," again.

"Religious reasons?"

"Please sir, I'm going to ask you—don't be offended, will you?—I'm going to ask you to leave because I have a meeting in five minutes."

I noticed another thing. How did the mayor know—aside from the fact that the bit about the meeting was nonsense—how did he know about the five minutes if he didn't have a watch nor were there clocks in the office nor in the whole municipality, nor in the home of Señora Ribkamatia who was in all certainty his cousin as well? How did he know? But I let it pass.

"That's fine," I said, "I'm leaving. But I imagine that if I can't sell medicines, I could sell iron fittings or plastic pipes or anilines."

"I don't know, I don't know," he said, and he pushed me toward the door. "I don't know, we'd have to see if they authorized us."

"If who authorized you?" I barked with the door already open and halfway into the corridor. "Aren't you the mayor here?"

"Yes, of course I am," the guy said, "tomorrow I'll give you an answer, come back tomorrow, all right?" and he closed the door in my face.

Of course, I left, what else was I going to do? I walked all over the city, which didn't take much time, looking at everything and remembering Edessbuss with fury and a little amusement, looking at the women's long hoopskirts; the men's clogs, smocks, and short pants; looking at a few who wore ruffs and plumed hats, others in cheap linen tunics and bare feet, looking at those who wore very short skins as their only clothing, all without knowing the reason for such a hodge-podge. They were probably foreigners. No one seemed very happy; not even the tourists, if that's what they were. I calculated where so many people might fit, because the city was much more populated that it had seemed. I thought there were very few houses for such a quantity of people, but that wasn't my affair. I wandered a little, concerned about the things that were my affair, because The Crazy Minstrel and The Splendorous Girl and The Empress and The Twelfth Knight had caught me in their snare but I didn't plan on leaving without having sold something—even though in the end what I did was give something—and giving Ribkamatia time to prepare the meal which, since I hadn't said anything, who knew if it would be meat or fish. In the middle of that, I came to the plaza and walked among the people who were selling things to see if there was some secret. If there was, I was going to find out: I have been buying and selling for twenty years and I know all the tricks. Almost all. I can assure you there was nothing unusual. They bought and sold as it's done everywhere, but only there in the market. There were no other shops or businesses. I pretended I wanted to buy a belt, and after haggling for a bit in the best style, I asked the owner of the stall how one went about getting a sales permit.

"The mayor, I don't know, you'd have to see if he can, I, of course, don't know, you understand," and he looked off in another direction.

I bought the belt from him, poor guy, in the end he was a colleague in unfortunate circumstances, and although the leather was shoddy and the buckle was twisted, he was asking peanuts. I paid and I went on walking, and on the other side of the plaza, I chose another stall at which to keep making inquiries. It was run by a girl selling lace, so beautiful. The girl, not the lace. She had chestnut hair tied in a bun at the nape of her neck and the prettiest ears I have ever seen—and look, it's not easy to find pretty ears, it's like with knees—and huge chestnut eyes and a spectacular figure evident under the long flowered skirt and very buttoned-up white blouse and the wide velvet belt with whalebone stays that was practically a vest tied with ribbons that crossed in front. I sidled up little by little and started looking at the lace, which interested me not one bit, until I got into a conversation with her and told her I was from elsewhere and what was her name and when I told her my last name she looked straight at me and said her last name was González, of course, and first name Inidiziba. I complimented her name and her eyes, and since I was there, her hands, too, but I couldn't bring myself to mention the ears, not that I didn't want to say something, but she didn't seem inclined to give me an in. Finally, after a lot of feints and a lot of verse, when I was about to say to hell with her, I got her to agree to meet me that night. "What time tonight?" I asked her, and I remembered about the clocks, or rather, the lack of clocks.

"When it's full night," she told me, as if that meant anything, "in the garden at my house," and she pointed out where that was and then she all but swept me out with the broom.

I won't say no, a good cup of coffee helps to get through anything, even the mess with the González family, and this coffee is running neck and neck with that prepared by Ribkamatia González, I assure you, and that is saying a lot. And how she cooked. From the lace-seller's stall I went straight to her house, where the table was already set. In the dining room and for me alone. I agreed to the dining room, although I was sure it was never used, but I refused to sit down unless she also sat down to eat with me. It was a splendid meal. Fish with vegetables. Simple, right? Let me tell you, it is like that, with the simple things, that you see the hand of the cook. A complicated dish is deceptive: at bottom there may be nothing more than a good recipe and a lot of patience. But if a baked fish with cooked vegetables is so good you could set it before His Most Serene Majesty the Emperor of China without danger of decapitation or hanging, then the cook is a sage and I tip my hat to her. I ate two helpings, I, who maintain that the best homage one can pay a meal is to leave the table hungry. And for dessert she served a sour cream with black sugar on top for which the Emperor would grant the title of Master of the Great Wall to anyone who gave him the privilege of tasting a mouthful. And I drank I don't know how many cups of coffee. While she went to wash the dishes, I asked her if she didn't have a newspaper to hand. She didn't understand me. A periodical, I said, and nothing. I told her what a newspaper was. As was to be expected, there were no newspapers on González. I deserved it and I said to myself that I must remember, next time I went to Edessbuss, to take a few kilos of bonbons filled with laxatives. It wouldn't be very subtle but it would correspond precisely to my mood and they, too, were going to deserve it, so there. So I went to take a siesta. I slept until six in the evening: I did have a watch. As I left my room, I heard Ribkamatia González talking with someone, with a man, in the front room, and it seemed to me that she was angry, very angry. I am discreet. Sometimes. I went back into the bedroom, I waited a few minutes, and then I came out again, making a lot of noise but you couldn't hear voices any longer and she asked me from the kitchen if I wanted a little coffee. What do you think I told her? We sat down beside a window, I to drink coffee and she to sew, and she asked me how the matter of the sales had gone. Of course, during the meal I had been so busy praising the food that I hadn't given her an account. I told her and I said we would see the next day, at the next meeting with the mayor. She sighed and said her cousin the mayor was a good person but he had no character, that's why he was mayor. It seemed to me a contradictory observation, but I didn't argue.

"It's a real disgrace, Señor Medrano," she said, "a real disgrace."

"That your cousin the mayor has no character?" I asked.

"No, no," she said without taking her eyes off her sewing. "I was speaking in general."

More than discreet, I think I am opportune. That's it, opportune. She was quiet for a moment and I didn't ask any questions because I sensed she was going to keep talking. She made a few stitches, cut the thread with a pair of scissors whose blades were very thin and very long, threaded the needle again and, of course, continued:

"Because, imagine everything one could do here, everything we could already have, because there's no shortage of capable people, with those kids who sacrifice themselves studying, investigating, inventing and trying things in secret."

I didn't know what she was talking about and she assumed I did, and I didn't ask that time either, not out of discretion but because I felt too peaceful and something was going to start to go badly if I stuck my foot in it.

"Lights," she said. "Electric lights—even atomic ones—automobiles, airplanes, injections, submarines, telephones, television, hospitals, sewing machines, all of that. And the only thing we can do is learn they exist on other worlds, thanks to what the wayward youth are able to find out and make known in secret." She looked at me. "They haven't been in contact with you yet?"

"Who?" I asked, like an idiot.

"The Wayward Youth," that time I heard it correctly, with capital letters.

She had gotten up to light two oil lamps.

"Ah," I said, a little unsteady, more even than the lamps' little flames. "No, no, not yet."

She went back to her sewing.

"You'll meet them. Poor people, they do everything they can."

She sewed a while longer, not speaking, and I didn't speak either. Afterward, she left the sewing and stood up. It was night, late at night.

"What would you like me to make you for supper?" she asked.

"Look, ma'am," I said, "leave me something light prepared, because I'm going to go out now and I don't know what time I'll be back."

"Ah," she said, with a knowing smile.

Afterward I learned she had not been thinking about the girl with the lace or about any girl, but in fact about those very Wayward Youth.

"I'm going to make you a stuffed egg," she said, and she went to the kitchen. A stuffed egg was taking my request for something light a little too literally, but it wasn't a hen's egg or an egg from an animal the size of a chicken, but a plasco egg. A plasco is an oviparous mammal similar to the farfarfa of Pilandeos VII, so imagine the size of that egg: I couldn't eat even half of it. But of course; oh yes, I'd be pleased if you'd join me. No, gastritis, never. The day I get gastritis I'll have to park the clunker for good. There are places where you can't go around choosing your food: on Emeterdelbe for example, either one digests the damned pies, sede pies, felepés pies, estelte pies, resne pies, pies made out of anything you can imagine, always fried in pelende fat, or one starves to death. And on Mitramm you have to have an iron stomach to tolerate the meat of the. I beg your pardon? Yes, I imagine so, I was intrigued, too. So I told her so long and she went to the door to say good-bye, with her cheeks red from the heat of the wood stove. It occurred to me that she must have been a beauty when she was young, not so long ago, and I gave her an approving look and as she was no fool she noticed and she laughed at me. Maybe she also laughed because she liked me looking at her that way. I left. I crossed the plaza in which, although it was already night, there were an enormous number of people who didn't seem to be doing anything. Everything was dark, save for a torch on a corner here and there. I carried a lantern and, of course, the Aqüivanida brake secured to my wrist. No, I call it the brake because of the effect it produces; they call it an apical molecular recensor, AMR. I arrived at the girl's house, turned around, hopped over the wall and went into the garden. No one seemed to be there. It was a neglected garden, not like Ribkamatia's, and I went behind a bush that was in urgent need of the pruning shears and waited. I almost fell asleep standing up. After half an hour, or more, I felt someone grabbing my arm. They must have crept up like a cat because I didn't hear any footsteps. In my fright I didn't manage to grab the lantern or the brake. But whoever it was let out a *tsk* at me: it was the beauty of the lace.

"Sweetheart," I said, "you step with more care than a fat tight-rope walker. I didn't hear you arrive."

She squeezed my arm again and went *tsk* and she led me by feel to a corner with a bench while I thought about how I should best begin, with the sentimental approach or with the clever questioning: it seemed to me best to combine information with pleasure. But it was no use on either front. On the pleasure side I couldn't, I won't even say take her to bed, which was what any normal guy would have wanted to do, I couldn't even touch the little finger of her left hand, because she was sullen, distrustful, a little stupid, and she was afraid. And on the information side, for those same reasons, she didn't want to tell me anything and she even suggested I was pulling her leg or wanted to make her fall into a trap. All I could find out was that she wouldn't let me get close or extol my undying love and that she didn't want to tell me anything because her grandfather, her grandmother, her great-grandfather, and above all her great-great-grandmother had forbidden it.

"Good lord!" I said. "What a long-lived family you have."

She got mad. She got so mad she even made noise when she got up from the bench and she told me to leave immediately. I couldn't convince her even by promising to maintain five meters of distance between us. Fine, I thought, to hell with her, her loss. I wasn't even interested anymore, I wanted a woman but I wouldn't have gone to bed with that fool for anything in the world. But I was more intrigued by the minute, and on that front, too, I had to go away hungry. The girl left me standing there and ran toward the house, and then I headed for the garden wall. And at that moment I saw we had not been alone: there was a great big woman with a viper's face, who couldn't be the great-great-grandmother because she wasn't that old, close to the place where I had been hidden, and two guys, one old enough to be her grandfather and another, younger one, and the three were watching me with hangman's eyes. I didn't wait to find out who they were or what they wanted. I jumped over the wall and left with all the rage in the world. The houses were dark and closed up but the streets and the plaza were full of silent people who came and went or sat on the benches or stood on the corners and looked around. Ribkamatia had left a small oil lamp burning in the hall. I picked it up and went to the kitchen where I attacked the plasco egg which was delicious but was too much for me: I never eat to excess and especially not before going to bed. That might be why I don't have gastritis. Then there was a noise of steps in the dark corridor and she appeared and said she had been waiting for me to set the table. I thanked her but told her she shouldn't do so again and we sat down in the kitchen and unstuffed what we could of the stuffed egg. She was dying of curiosity but she didn't ask me anything and I was in no mood to tell her about the let-down I had suffered. She made me coffee and I drank it and I felt better. I said I was going to bed and she stood up. I picked up the lamp and set off toward the bedroom. I opened the door, I wished her goodnight, and right there I did the best thing I had done in a long time: I lifted the little oil lamp to see her better and caressed her face with my free hand. She gave me a sweet smile. I don't like adjectives but the smile was sweet, what can I say, sweet and placid. She opened the door to her room and I wasn't going to be so slow-witted as to go into mine. Yes, I slept with her, in as much as I slept, which was just enough. No lace seller, no girl as splendorous as she might be, no amazon, no big woman bored with her old husband, no adolescent or queen of eight kingdoms or professional or slave or actress or hungry conspirator or anything, not one have I found, I remember no one who knew as well as she what a man wanted in bed—not a macho, a man. From what there was between the two of us those nights, we could have been married for years and years and could have gone to bed together hundreds of times, each one like the first or second time, and everything was always going to go well and there was nothing to worry about. Why is it that I don't like to talk about her much? It was almost dawn when I fell sound asleep and it seemed to me that not even five minutes had passed but it must have been late because the sun was starting to come through the cracks in the shutters when a noise and a shout woke me up. I sat up in bed and saw a guy standing in the open doorway, his face twisted and contorted with rage. Ribkamatia opened her eyes but she wasn't frightened: she just looked at him as if to say ugh, here you come to screw things up again while the jerk breathed heavily with his hand on the door handle. She said very calmly:

"And now what is it?"

He insulted her at length but without using a single word the archbishop of Santiago de Compostela couldn't have used on a Maundy Thursday afternoon. He reminded me of a priest who taught us religion when I was a boy. I was, as you will understand, at a disadvantage: naked, half asleep, in a strange house and a strange bed and without knowing what right the shouter had to come into the bedroom. I didn't like him calling her filthy sinner and other things of a biblical ilk so I stood up and insulted him but without watching my language, on the contrary. The guy paid no attention to me, it seemed the issue was with her, and so much so that he came close to the bed and made a move to strike her. Oh no, my friend, in front of me, no: if someone wants to hit a girl and the girl is stupid enough to let him, it doesn't matter to me, but not if I'm around, because then you've started something. I grabbed him by the shoulder, I made him turn around, and I landed a punch. He stumbled and came right at me. He was shorter and stockier than I, but if he was mad, I was madder. I landed a couple of good blows and faked with another to the face trying to make him cover so as to hit him in the gut, knock him to the ground and kick him in the head. Yes, I was furious and when I'm furious, I'm no gentleman in the ring. He was furious, too, obviously, but on the theological side, and there's nothing like theology to sap the effectiveness of your punches, so I looked likely to win. He saw that and snatched up the long scissors that were on the dresser and lunged at me. He was no gentleman in the ring either, I am sorry to say, may he rest in peace. I grabbed him by the wrist, twisted it until it cracked, and took away the scissors. He threw himself on top of me—he didn't lack courage—and I parried with my right but I had the scissors in that hand. I buried them up to the handle in his chest and the guy fell down. I was stunned. Even more so when I looked at Ribkamatia, thinking I would find her half fainting, pale and covering her mouth with her hand, and I saw she was just fine: irritated, I'd say, impatient, but not scared. I may have killed at some time or another, I'm not saying no and I'm not saying yes, either, but if I believe in anything, I believe in the *non possumus*. For a second, I shouldered all the sins of all those sentenced to eternal punishment, and the next second, when I looked at the guy dead on the floor, I saw him stand up, almost as if nothing had happened except for the scissors driven in at the level of his heart, and I saw how he yanked them out without leaving a hint of the wound, with no wound—do you understand?—and how he dusted off his shirt and pants and how he put the scissors on the dresser and left, looking backward and muttering things, more insults I think, although I didn't hear him. The door closed and I sat down on the edge of the bed.

"That imbecile never learns," Ribkamatia said, and she ran her hand over my head.

"Who is it?" I asked.

"My husband," she said.

I looked at her, so pretty and fresh, so pretty: "But aren't you a widow? Isn't your husband dead?"

"Of course he's dead," she said, "and I have already told him a thousand times I'm not a coward and no one's going to keep ordering me around, not him or anyone."

"Ribka," I said to her, feeling suddenly perfectly calm, "I want you to explain to me how a dead man can be alive and come to fight with his widow's lover."

"He's just like all of them," she said, "he can't help it, poor thing."

"All of the dead are alive," I said.

"They're dead but it's as if they were alive," and she looked at me for a while without saying anything. "Then, you didn't know?"

"No," I said. "You thought I knew, but no. Who are the Wayward Youth? What are the dead? Zombies? Vampires? Why is there no electricity, no clocks? Are all of those walking around the streets dead? Why can't I sell medicines?"

She laughed. She put her arms around me, she made me lie down again next to her and she told me. On González people died just as they do anywhere, but they didn't stay deceased and quiet in the coffin like the polite departed. There weren't even coffins. Or niches or pantheons or cemeteries or funeral parlors. What for? The dead got up just a little while after having died and devoted themselves to messing with the living. They died, no joking: their hearts stopped and their blood didn't circulate and there were no more vital functions, but there they were, in the streets, in the plaza, in the countryside, moving into the family home from time to time or going off who knows where. Only they weren't different solely physiologically. They were different due to anger or resentment, due to death: they wanted things to continue as they were when they were alive and for that reason they wanted the living to live like the dead. They didn't allow anything to happen that might alter the life they had known. With their common ancestors always among them, like someone who has a deaf great-aunt living in their attic, it was logical that they all continued being part of the same family, and they were all cousins and they were all named González. Of course, as there were very ancient dead, the monkey faces wrapped up in skins, but there were also more recent dead, the new ones compromised on a few things that in their turn, when they were alive, they had managed to impose against the wishes or the orders of the dead they had had to put up with. That's why there was running water, for example. But there weren't doctors or hospitals or medicines, because the dead wanted the living to join the dead as soon as possible. And the less romance there was, the better; fewer marriages, although what romance has to do with marriage is something I haven't managed to comprehend, unless it's a risk one has to know how to avoid, but the dead have a very particular idea in that respect: fewer offspring, fewer of the living. In sum, González was on the path to being a world of the dead. I was getting to that: hundreds of thousands of years ago, a comet passed by and the tail grazed González and it seems it liked the neighborhood because it returns every five years. I don't remember what the comet was called or if it had a name: probably not, because it didn't have a name the first time it passed. Every five years it renews the phenomenon of the suppression of some of the characteristics of death—rotting decorously, for example, and not appearing again unless it's at the three-legged table of some charlatan. At least that was the explanation Ribka gave me and that everyone accepted as valid. There doesn't seem to be another: there must be something in the tail of that comet and I have no interest in finding out what it is. I can't imagine God the Father decreeing that the dead of González have to keep on screwing over the living for all eternity. The Wayward Youth? The ones who talk back and disobey dad and mom, the rebels, the ones who conspire—and you will recognize that it's not easy—against the dead. A clandestine organization, but not really, because you can't do anything entirely hidden from so many dead among whom some were Wayward Youth when they were alive: an organization that made plans, favored study, resistance, research, and curiosity. They flew in balloons—remember?—for coordination and information from city to city, but in secret. Every time the dead found a balloon, they destroyed it. I had caught one they hadn't managed to land before it got light and it had seemed to me as if it was camouflaged. It was camouflaged. No, of course not, the dead weren't supermen, they didn't have any other faculties than those they'd had when alive: they couldn't prevent people arriving from elsewhere, but they could oblige some of the living, the wimps as Ribka called them, not to give them the time of day, or lodge them, or give them food or provide them with anything. Those who arrived left again as soon as possible. But the Wayward Youth managed to talk with them and have news of what there was on other worlds. Well, the dead threatened the living that they'd kill them if they didn't obey. It seems, nonetheless, that they couldn't do it, that a dead person had never killed one of the living, otherwise González would have been peopled with the dead centuries ago. It's possible they couldn't. But just in case, the living obeyed. Not all of them: observe Ribka and the Wayward Youth. And the living didn't want to join the dead, one because nobody likes to die and two because they knew what they would become. You see, the perfect fear. Yes, those strange people in the street were dead and those I met in the lace girl's garden were dead. The not-so-old woman was the great-great-grandmother who had died at thirty-seven and the oldest old guy was the grandfather who had died at seventy-six. Many of the living let themselves be controlled by the dead, like the mayor and the lace girl and Ribka's neighbor. But others did not. They fought—so far as they were able, but they fought. And I, who as my friend Jorge says—he's a poet but a good guy—I am a romantic and my chest throbs achingly at certain things; I, who had spent with Ribka the loveliest night of my life, I entered the bullring to fight, too. I sat up in bed and I said:

"Ribka, we are going to make love again, because I like to make love in the morning and I like to make love and I like it with you, and then we are going to bathe together and drink coffee together and we are going to get ourselves gussied up and we are going to go look for the Wayward Youth, but first we are going to go by the clunker."

I liked the way she laughed. Is there a bit more coffee? Thank you. This, too, may be an imposition but the occasion requires it, telling these things. When we went out to the street, cousin González was in the doorway of his house and I went up to him, I gave him my hand and I said hello, how are you, nice morning, don't you think? And he looked at me as if I had gone crazy and Ribka and I walked off together. I don't only carry merchandise on my trips. I take some of everything—if I tell you, I'll never finish. I opened the clunker and we went in and started to rummage around. I gave her two clocks, a wristwatch for her to wear and a clock for her home, and I wrapped up a big clock for the municipality because the government, even if it's municipal, has to provide an example. She wasn't afraid and she was going to use them, but I told her to put the big one away, she wouldn't have to keep it hidden very long. I gave her a short, yellow silk dress, very low cut and sleeveless, which I had asked a friend from Sinderastie to buy for me so as to give it to the daughter of a businessman on Dosirdoo IX to whom I owe attentions. I gave her an electric mixer, promising her she would be able to use it. No, I wasn't sure yet, but it was reasonable to think so and, above all, I wanted to believe it. And I gave her a diamond from Quitiloe. Maybe she has sold it by now as I advised her and has gone on a luxury vacation cruise to Edessbuss and Naijale II and Ossawo. Or maybe she has kept it because I gave it to her. I like both possibilities. Then, loaded down with the packages, we went, in the most roundabout way, to a house on the outskirts of the city, where the Wayward Youth were meeting that day. She was in contact with them. She wasn't part of the organization, because she was too independent and didn't accept directives from the dead or from the living, but she knew all the places they met, which, as a precaution, changed every day. From time to time the dead found them, but in general they managed quite well. Good people, a few of them desperate but all of them hardheaded and fighters. Ribka told them about me and it turned out that very morning they had been looking for me in the city. I told them I needed to talk to them, the more of them the better, and that for once not to worry about the dead. They arranged to call all those they could and by midday there was a significant group, it almost looked like a demonstration. I climbed up on a table and said—quickly, because the lookouts told us the dead were already approaching—what had occurred to me. They got the idea right away and soon there was an infernal din. I tried to calm them but it was very difficult and then I thought, what do I care, it's the first time they've been happy. And I hoped it wouldn't be the last. The dead arrived and started to snoop around and make threats, but the atmosphere had changed. No one paid them much attention except for a few kids who yelled things at them, not exactly compliments. What hope can do, my God. They had become, I won't say brave because that they had always been, but spirited and even happy. Ribka went home, I kissed her and told her good-bye, and I went to the clunker with a delegation of the Wayward Youth. I took off toward Edessbuss. And there we arrived, in full Carnival celebration. Those who were finishing their work shift in the port, put on their masks and their Zorro or Invincible Buccaneer costumes, grabbed the streamers and the perfume-sprayers and went to dance. It was a hassle trying to locate The Crazy Minstrel of the Still Waters but after traipsing through a dozen parties, we bet on his house and we waited for him there. He arrived with an odalisque and a Hungarian ballerina, very pretty, very heavily made-up, but no comparison to Ribka. Yes, he was surprised to see me, but he received me as friends are received on Edessbuss. Right there I told him I was going to make him pay for the nasty joke about selling medicines on González. To start, he had to put me in contact with the people in charge of the Roof. The poor thing, completely canned, dressed as a robot, didn't understand much, but I introduced him to the Wayward Youth and told him they needed a few reports. Urgently, I said. We went in. He dressed, he changed, the two girls flopped down to sleep on a sofa and we left. For the Superior Institute of Technology and Environmental Protection. There, in front of a number of very agreeable individuals who were not in costume but who, I'd bet my life on it, had been until midnight at least, we laid out the case of González, which all of them knew, some of them well, others better or worse. And I proposed the solution, trembling—what if they told me it couldn't be done? But they said yes. They not only said yes but they got excited about it and began to ring bells calling engineers, project designers, calculators, ecologists, and I don't know who all else and an hour later they were drawing and making calculations like crazy. I won't take up more of your time: the next day we returned to González, and behind my clunker—the poor thing looked like a rickety guide fish leading three giant sharks—came three heavy cruisers full of technicians, workmen, and building material. On González I went to Ribka's house and I washed my hands of the affair. I made love with her that morning, that afternoon, and that night, and all the following nights, but after the first night, I had to convince her to take off the wristwatch because my back was covered in scratches. No, the husband didn't appear. Not because he was afraid of me: the dead of González have no fear or anything; he must have been busy with the other dead trying to prevent the technicians from Edessbuss from doing their work. My friend, you can imagine that if the Edessbussianos have placed a cover over their own world, it's easy enough for them to extend another around their camps and their men if they don't want anyone to bother them. And I had the Aqüivanida brake, don't forget. With the brake I neutralized half a dozen attempts, that would have come to nothing anyway, by the González dead against the González living and from then on the worthy forebears stayed in their place and resigned themselves to being like the dead on other worlds. The brake also worked on the dead for just that reason, the lack of metabolism. A week. Yes, it took them no more than a week to wrap González in an anti-comet tail, not anti-energy, Roof. After the week they left, leaving everything ready, and González sang and danced for the first time in a million years. I left, too. It would be two years before the comet passed again. If the tail didn't touch González, and it wasn't going to touch because the Edessbussianos swore that any comet's tail was a joke next to the energy of Edess-Pálida, the dead were going to die for real and along with those who would die later, they would feed the worms and geraniums like any self-respecting dead person, in nice and orderly cemeteries full of cypress trees and ostentatious plaques and healthy sobbing. Before I lifted off, I saw the first sparkle of the Roof that was already functioning. I imagine it's still working. I imagine the dead will have gradually disappeared. I imagine Ribka has an electric sewing machine and a twelve-bulb chandelier in the dining room, that she uses the mixer and the watch, the clocks. I imagine the great-great-grandmother is no longer there to guard the virginity of the lace girl. I imagine there are airplanes and aspirin. I imagine that Ribka remembers me. Yes, thank you, I never say no to such good coffee.

Interval with my Aunts

Trafalgar and Josefina

to the memory of my aunts

*Paula, Rosario, Elisa
and Carmencita.
and to my aunts Laura, Manena,
Virginia and Pilar.*

My Aunt Josefina came to visit me. He who has never met my Aunt Josefina doesn't know what he's missing, as Trafalgar Medrano says. Trafalgar also says that she is one of the most beautiful and charming women he has met and that if he had been born in 1893 he would not have married her for anything in the world. My aunt came in, she looked the house over and asked after the children, she wanted to know if I was ever going to decide to move to an apartment downtown, and when I said no, never, she hesitated over whether or not to leave her jacket somewhere and decided to take it with her because there might be a little breeze in the garden later. She's eighty-four years old; wavy hair the color of steel, a couple of tireless chestnut eyes as bright as they say my *criolla* great-grandmother's were, and an enviable figure: if she wanted to, if she went so far as to admit that those coarse and disagreeable things should be used as items of clothing, she could wear Cecilia's jeans. She said the garden was lovely and that it would look much better when we had the ash trees pruned and the tea was delicious and she loved scones but they turned out better with only one egg.

"I drank a very good tea the other day. Yes, I am going to have a little more but half a cup, that's good, don't get carried away. Isn't it a little strong? Just one little drop of milk. That's it. And they served me some very good toast, with butter and not that rancid margarine they give you now everywhere, I don't know how you can like it. In the Burgundy. And I was with a friend of yours."

"I already know," I said. "Trafalgar."

"Yes, the son of Juan José Medrano and poor Merceditas. I don't understand how she allowed her only son to be given that outlandish name. Well, I always suspected Medrano was a Mason."

"But Josefina, what does Freemasonry have to do with the Battle of Trafalgar?"

"Ah, I don't know, sweetie, but you can't deny that the Masons purposely gave their children names that didn't appear in the calendar of saints."

"Doctor Medrano was probably an admirer of Nelson," I said, pinning all my hopes on Trafalgar's old man's interest in the great events of history.

"What I can assure you," said my Aunt Josefina, "is that Merceditas Herrera was a saint, and so refined and discreet."

"And Doctor Medrano, what was he like?"

"A great doctor," she opened another scone and spread orange marmalade on it. "Good-looking and congenial as well. And very cultured."

There was a quarter-second silence before the last statement: the word *cultured* is slippery with my Aunt Josefina and one has to step carefully.

"Trafalgar is also good-looking and congenial," I said, "but I don't know if he's cultured. He knows a ton of strange things."

"It's true, he's congenial, very congenial and friendly. And very considerate with an old lady like me. Now, I think good-looking is an exaggeration. His nose is too long, just like poor Merceditas'. And don't tell me that mustache isn't a little ridiculous. A man looks much tidier if clean-shaven, thank goodness your sons have gotten over the beard and mustache phase. But I have to admit that the boy is elegant: he had on a dark gray suit, very well cut, and a white shirt and a serious tie, not like some of your extravagant friends who look like. I don't even know what they look like."

"Would you like a little more tea?"

"No, no, please, you've already made me drink too much, but it was delicious and I have overdone it. That was Thursday or Friday, I'm not sure. I went into the Burgundy because I was fainting with hunger: I was coming from a meeting of the board of directors of the Society of Friends of the Museum, so it was Thursday, of course, because Friday was the engagement party of María Luisa's daughter, and you know Thursday is Amelia's afternoon off, and frankly I had no desire to go home and start making tea. There weren't many people and I sat down far away from the door, where there wouldn't be a draft, and when they were serving my tea the Medrano boy came in. He came over to say hello, so kind. At first I couldn't place him and I was about to ask him who he was when I realized he was Merceditas Herrera's son. It was so unsettling, seeing him standing there beside the table, but although I am old enough to do certain things, you understand that a lady never invites a man, even though he's *so* much younger than she is, to sit at her table."

An "Oh, no?" escaped me.

My Aunt Josefina sighed, I would almost say she blew out air, and great-grandmother's eyes stopped me cold.

"I do know customs have evolved," she said, "and in a few cases for the better, and in many others unfortunately for the worse, but there are things that do not change and you should know that."

I smiled because I love her a lot and because I hope I can get to eighty-four years old with the same confidence she has and learn to control my eyes the way she does although mine aren't even a tenth as pretty.

"And you let poor Trafalgar go?"

"No. He was very correct and he asked my permission to keep me company if I wasn't waiting for anyone. I told him to sit down and he ordered coffee. It's appalling how that boy drinks coffee. I don't know how he doesn't ruin his stomach. I haven't tasted coffee in years."

She doesn't smoke either, of course. And she drinks a quarter glass of rosé with every dinner and another quarter glass, only of extra-dry champagne, at Christmas and New Year's.

"He didn't tell you if he was going to come by here?"

"No, he didn't say, but it seems unlikely. He was going, I think the next day, I'm not really sure where, it must be Japan, I imagine, because he said he was going to buy silks. A shame he devotes himself to commerce and didn't follow his father's path: it was a disappointment to poor Merceditas. But he's doing very well, isn't he?"

"He's doing fabulously. He has truckloads of dough."

"I sincerely hope you don't use that language outside your home. It is unbecoming. Of course, it would be best if you never used it, but that's evidently hopeless. You're as stubborn as your father."

"Yes, my old man, I mean my father, was stubborn, but he was a gentleman."

"True. I don't know how he spoke when he was among other men, that doesn't matter, but he never said anything inappropriate in public."

"If you heard Trafalgar talk, you'd have an attack."

"I don't see why. With me, he was most agreeable. Neither affected nor hoity-toity—no need for that—but very careful."

"He's a hypocritical cretin." That I didn't say, I just thought it.

"And he has," said my Aunt Josefina, "a special charm for telling the most outlandish things. What an imagination."

"What did he tell you?"

"Obviously, maybe it's not all imagination. It gives you the impression that he is telling the truth, but so embellished that at first glance you could think it was a big lie. I'll tell you I spent a very entertaining interval. How is it possible that when I arrived home Amelia was already back and was worried at my delay? The poor thing had called Cuca's house, and Mimi's and Virginia's to see if I was there. I had to start in on the phone calls to calm them all down."

I got serious: I was dying of envy, like when Trafalgar goes and tells things to Fatty Páez or Raúl or Jorge. But I understood, because my Aunt Josefina knows how to do many things well; for example, to listen.

"What did he tell you?"

"Oh, nothing, crazy things about his trips. Of course, he speaks so well that it's a pleasure, a real pleasure."

"What did he tell you?"

"Sweetie, how you insist! Besides, I don't remember too well."

"Yeah, tell me what you remember."

"One says 'yes,' not 'yeah.' You sound like a muleteer, not a lady."

I ignored her.

"Of course you remember. You catch cold with a constancy worthy of a greater cause and your stomach is a little fragile, but don't tell me you have arteriosclerosis, because I won't believe you."

"God preserve me. Have you seen Raquel lately? A fright. She was at the Peñas', I don't know why they take her, and she didn't recognize me."

"Josefina, I am going to go crazy with curiosity. Be nice and tell me what Trafalgar told you."

"Let's see, wait, I'm not really sure."

"For certain he told you he had just arrived from somewhere."

"That's it. It must be one of those new countries in Africa or Asia, with a very strange name I have never heard before or ever read in the newspaper. What surprised me was that they were so advanced, with so much progress and so well organized, because they always turn savage: look what happened in India when the English left and in the Congo after the Belgians, no? Your friend Medrano told me it was a world—a world, that's what he said—that was very attractive when one saw it for the first time. Serprabel, now I remember, Serprabel. I think it must be close to India."

"I doubt it but, anyway, go on."

"Nevertheless, almost certainly, yes, it must be near India, not only because of the name but because of the castes."

"What castes?"

"Aren't there castes in India?"

"Yes, there are, but what does that have to do with it?"

"If you let me tell you, you're going to find out; weren't you in such a big hurry? And sit properly, it's so obvious you are all used to wearing pants. There are no elegant women anymore."

"Tell me, in Serprabel, are there elegant women?"

"Yes, according to the Medrano boy, there are splendid women, very well dressed and very well bred."

"It doesn't surprise me; even if there's only one, he'll find her."

"A shame he never married."

"Who? Trafalgar?" I laughed for a while.

"I don't see what's funny about it. I'm not saying with a foreigner, and from so far away, who may be a very good person, but have different customs, but with someone from his circle. Don't forget, he comes from a very well-connected family."

"That one's going to die an old bachelor. He likes women too much."

"Hmmmmm," went my Aunt Josefina.

"Don't tell me Medrano Senior did, too!" I exclaimed.

"Be discreet, sweetheart, don't talk so loud. In fact, I can't confirm anything. A few things were said at the time."

"I can imagine," I said. "And Merceditas was a saint. And on Serprabel Trafalgar was looking for romance, just as his father would have been."

"But how can you think that? He wasn't looking for romance, as you say. And if he were, he wouldn't have told me. One can see he is a very polite boy. What he did, or what he says he did, because it was most likely nothing more than a story to entertain me for a while, what he did was to try to help a poor woman, who was very unfortunate for many reasons."

"Ay," I said, and once again thought that Trafalgar was a hypocritical cretin.

"Now what's the matter?"

"Nothing, nothing, go on."

"Well, it seems that there they maintain—following those eastern religions, no?—a caste system. And there are nine. Let's see, let me think: lords, priests, warriors, scholars, merchants, artisans, servants, and vagabonds. Oh, no, eight. They're eight."

"And everyone has to be in one of the castes."

"Of course. Don't tell me it isn't an advantage."

"Oh, I don't know. What does one do if one is an artisan and has the vocation to be a merchant, like Trafalgar? Do they take an exam?"

"Of course not. Everyone lives within the caste to which they belong and they marry people from their own caste."

"Don't tell me: and their children are born within that caste and die within that caste and the children of those children and so on forever."

"Yes. So no one has pretentions and everyone stays in their place and they avoid disorders and revolutions and strikes. I said to Medrano that, paganism aside, it seemed to me an extraordinary system and he agreed with me."

"Ah, he agreed with you."

"Of course, he even told me that in thousands of years there had never been any disorder and they had lived in peace."

"How nice."

"I know it must sound a little old-fashioned to you, but Medrano says the level of development in everything, color television and airlines and telephones with a view screen and computer centers, is impressive. I'm surprised they don't advertise more to attract tourism. I myself, if I were inclined to travel at my age, would be very happy to go for a visit. Listen, he says the hotels are extraordinary and the service is perfect, the food is delicious, and there are museums and theaters and places to visit and splendid, just splendid landscapes."

"I don't like that caste thing. I wouldn't go even at gunpoint."

"Nor I, believe me, I would not enjoy such a long plane trip. But the caste thing is not that important, because anyone can govern."

"What did you say?"

"That anyone can govern. Above everyone is a kind of king who lives in the center of the capital, because the city is a circle and in the middle is the Palace which is all marble and gold and crystal. Anyway, that's what your friend says. I don't doubt that it's very luxurious, but not that much."

"And anyone can become king? I mean, everything else is hereditary and that, specifically, is not?"

"That's what Medrano told me. So you see, if the highest authority can be elected, everything is very democratic. The king is called the Lord of Lords and governs for a period of five years; when it's over, he can't be reelected, he goes back home and then the Lords elect another."

"Wait, wait. The Lords? So then the others don't vote?"

"Nobody votes, sweetie. The Lords meet every five years and elect a Lord of Lords and look how nice, they almost always, or always, elect him from among the inferior castes, you see?"

"Heck yes, I see. And the Lord of Lords governs everybody?"

"I suppose so, that's what he's elected for. Although your friend Medrano says no, he doesn't govern."

"I thought so."

"Oh, sure, if he says it, it's holy writ."

"Fine, but what is it he says?"

Another of my Aunt Josefa's virtues is that she can't lie: "He says he's a puppet of the Lords who are the ones who really govern, so as to keep everyone happy with the illusion that they or someone of their caste might become king, but that the Lord of Lords is the ultimate slave, a slave who lives like a king, eats like a king, dresses like a king, but is still a slave."

And one of her defects consists in believing only what she wants to believe: "You see that can't be. Surely the Lords form a kind of Council or Chamber or something like that and your friend took one thing for another. Or he probably invented it to spice up the story."

"Yes, just probably. I warn you, Trafalgar is capable of anything."

"He also told me, this seems more reasonable to me, that the inferior castes are the more numerous. There is only one Lord of Lords. There are very few Lords, I think he told me there are a hundred. A few more Priests, many more, I think around three hundred. Many more Warriors and even more Scholars, he didn't tell me how many. Many, many Merchants, Artisans, and Servants, especially Servants. And it seems there are millions of Vagabonds. It must be a very populous country. And anyone of any caste, except the Lord of Lords, of course, can be Owner or Dispossessed."

"Having money or not having money? Rich and poor, let's say."

"More or less: he who has land is an Owner; he who does not is Dispossessed. And within each caste anyone who is an Owner is superior to the Dispossessed."

"And can one go from being Dispossessed to Owner?"

"Yes, so you already see that it's not as terrible as you thought. If one puts together enough money, one buys land, which is very expensive, just like everywhere. It seems to be a very rich country."

"The Vagabonds can buy land, too?"

"No, no. The Vagabonds are vagabonds. They don't even have houses, I don't know how people can live like that."

"I don't understand. Now tell me what happened to Trafalgar on Serprabel."

"It's a little cool, don't you think?"

"Do you want to go inside?"

"No, but help me put the jacket over my shoulders," not that my Aunt Josefina needs help to put on her jacket. "That's it, thank you. According to him, some of everything happened. He went there to sell jewelry and perfumes. He says he didn't do too well with the perfumes because they have a good chemical industry and flowers, you should see the flowers he described to me, very heavily scented ones from which they make extracts. But as there are no deposits of precious stones, he sold the ones he took very well. Of course, he had a few problems, believe me, because anyone who goes to Serprabel has to become part of a caste. They considered him a merchant and he had to use vehicles for Merchants and go to a hotel for Merchants. But when he learned that there were superior castes with better hotels and more privileges, he protested and said he was also a Scholar and a Warrior. He did the right thing, don't you think? Of course, since there one can't belong to more than one caste, they had to hold a kind of audience presided over by one of the Lords who had the strangest name, that I'm really not going to be able to remember, and there he explained his case. Oh, he made me laugh so much telling me how he had disconcerted them and remarking that he was very sorry he couldn't say he was a Lord, and that he would also have liked to say he was a Priest, which is the second caste. The bad part was he didn't know anything about the religion and he doesn't have mystical inclinations. Although I think he was educated in a religious school."

"That he has no mystical inclinations remains to be seen. So what happened?"

"They accepted that in other places there were other customs and they reached an agreement. He would be a Warrior but one of the lowest, those of the Earth, although an Owner, and with permission to act as a Merchant."

"What's that about those of the Earth?"

"Well, each one of the four superior castes has categories. For example, let's see, how was it, the Lords can be of Light, of Fire, and of Shadow, I think that was the order. The Priests can devote themselves to Communication, Intermediation, or Consolation. The Warriors act in the Air, the Water, or on the Earth. And the Scholars are dedicated to Knowledge, Accumulation, or Teaching. The others are inferior and don't have categories."

"What a mess. And each one can also be Owner or Dispossessed and that influences their position?"

"Yes. It's a little complicated. Medrano told me that a Lord of Light, an Owner, was the highest rank. And a Warrior of Air but Dispossessed was almost equal to a Priest devoted to Consolation but an Owner. Understand?"

"Not really. Anyway, they gave Trafalgar a very passable rank."

"He was very satisfied. The took him to a very superior hotel and that's even though he says the Merchants' hotel was very good, and they set four people to attend him exclusively, aside from the hotel personnel. The fact that he had jewels to sell also must have had some influence, because they are a real luxury. He says a delegation of Merchants went to see him and that although they couldn't enter the hotel, which was solely for Warriors, they spoke in the park and offered him a very well located shop where he could sell what he had brought. A few wanted to buy one or another piece of jewelry so as to sell it themselves but they were very expensive and the Merchants, although they aren't exactly poor, aren't rich, either. Only one of them, who was an Owner, and of a lot of land, might have been able to buy something from him, but Medrano didn't want to sell him anything; he did well, because why make such a long trip and end up splitting the profits with another? In any event they had to give him the location even though they didn't end on very friendly terms, because every caste has its laws and among the Merchants one can't go back after having offered something verbally or any other way, but above all verbally. Another law for all of the castes—which frankly, I don't know what result it would produce—seems very silly to me, it says no one can repeat to those of his own caste nor to those of other castes something he has overheard a member of another caste say, although they can repeat what members of their own caste have said. Of course this is hard to control, and no one speaks gladly to someone from another caste but only out of obligation, but every so often they catch an offender and the punishments are terrible; anyway, I don't know if it's really worth all that."

"But listen, more than silly, that's dangerous, because it's very vague, there aren't any limits. If you take it literally, no one can talk to anyone from another caste."

"There's something of that, as I said. But as the Lords, who are very intelligent and very fair, act as judges, there are no abuses. What is happening is that from caste to caste, the language is becoming more and more different. I forgot to ask Medrano what language they spoke and if he understood it. Would it be some dialect of Hindi? In any case, with a little English one can make oneself understood anywhere in the world."

"Trafalgar speaks excellent English. I expect he sold the jewelry."

"To the Lords, of course. The store fronts, the shops, those are public places where anyone can go, except for the Vagabonds who can't go anywhere, but when a Lord or a number of Lords enter, everyone else has to leave. Those that aren't Lords, because those that are Lords can stay. In any case, a crowd of people paraded through to see what Medrano had brought."

"I'd bet a year's paychecks he sold it all."

"I don't know what you were going to live on because he didn't sell everything. He had a pearl necklace left over."

"I don't believe you. No. Impossible. Never."

"Seriously. Of course it was because of everything that happened and anyway he was the one who decided to leave it, but he didn't sell it."

"I don't understand any of this, but it seems very unusual in Trafalgar."

"Well, the Lord of Lords governing at that time, and who had been elected by the Lords less than a year before, was a man not at all well-suited to the office. Listen, he had been a Vagabond, how awful."

"Why? Don't they elect the inferior castes as king?"

"Yes, of course, but seldom Vagabonds, who are illiterate and don't know how to eat or how to behave. But Medrano says they had elected him because he had the face and the poise of a king."

"High-class liars, those Lords."

"Sweetie, so vulgar."

"Don't tell me they aren't a bunch of liars and something worse, too."

"I don't think so, because from what Medrano told me they are irreproachable people. And it seems to me very democratic to elect a Vagabond as king. Even a bit idealistic, like something out of a novel."

"A cock-and-bull story."

"The fact is, the poor Lords made a mistake. Of course, an ignorant person, without education—what could you expect?"

"He left them in a bad state."

"He fell in love, can you believe, with a married woman."

"A Vagabond?"

"No, I think the Vagabonds don't even get married. Worse: he fell in love with the wife of a Scholar, and one of the best, the ones devoted to Knowledge and who for that reason was often at court. And Medrano found that out because he heard the Lords discussing what had to be done in the jewelry store he had opened. But as he didn't know that one can't repeat what members of a caste that isn't your own have said, and he was—at least so long as he was there—a Warrior, he mentioned it to a Scholar in conversation. I don't remember what category he belonged to, but Medrano says he had been looking at the jewels and that he was a very interesting man who knew a great deal about philosophy, mathematics, music, and it was worthwhile listening to him speak. He couldn't buy anything: only the Lords had picked up a lot of things, because the prices were very high for those of other castes, but he stayed until quite late, and as the two were alone and they had talked about the cutting of stones and of goldsmithing and of music, they started to talk about other things, too, and Medrano praised the country and the city and the other asked if he had seen the gardens at the Palace and they talked about the Lord of Lords and there your friend committed an indiscretion."

"He mentioned the Lord of Lords' affair with the woman."

"He said he had heard the Lords talk about that and he didn't realize he had said something he should not: he was just surprised when the Scholar became very serious and stopped talking and said good-bye very coldly and left."

"Trafalgar acts like a know-it-all but he never learns. He always sticks his foot in it."

"My goodness, what a way to speak."

"I promise to be more refined, or at least try to, but tell me what happened to him."

"When you want to you can speak correctly. The thing would be for you to always want to. That day, nothing happened to him. The next day he sold what he had left, only to the Lords, save for a pearl necklace that must have been beautiful, truly beautiful: a very long string of pink pearls all the same size. Natural pearls, as you can imagine. It must have cost a fortune."

"That was the one he left?"

"Yes, but wait. When he had nothing left but that necklace and was about to sell it to a Lord, the police came in and arrested him."

"It looks like there are police on Serprabel."

"Why not? They belong to the Servants caste. And they took him directly to the Palace of the Lord of Lords. There he had to wait, always under guard, with the necklace in his pocket, until they made him enter—shoved him, he says, how unpleasant—enter a courtroom. As repeating things said by someone from another caste is a serious crime, the judge wasn't just any Lord but the Lord of Lords. Of course, assisted by two Lords. The one who acted as prosecutor was another Lord, who put forward the accusation."

"And defender? Did he have a defender?"

"No, he had to defend himself. I will say it does not seem fair to me."

"Not fair at all. A filthy trick, forgive the term."

"It may be a little strong, but you're right. They accused him and he defended himself as well as he could. But note, they had to say what it was about, what it was Medrano had repeated. And it was nothing less than the illicit affairs of the very king presiding over the tribunal."

"Poor guy, my God."

"That boy really had a bad time."

"No, I mean the Lord of Lords."

"He had it coming, and don't think I don't feel sorry for him. But a person of quality does not stoop to such things."

"Oh, no, of course, why don't you read Shakespeare and Sophocles?"

"That may be all very well for the theater, but in real life it is not suitable. And things got worse when, after the accusation and the defense, the prosecutor detailed Medrano's crime and the Lord of Lords, who until then had been very much in his role, very serious and dignified and quiet on his throne, stood up and started to speak. It was not the conduct expected of a king, because everyone, and above all the Lords, Medrano explained to me, everyone was so scandalized that they couldn't do anything. They were frozen with their mouths open, staring at him."

"And what did he say?"

"A speech."

"A speech?"

"A parody of a speech. Medrano says he didn't even know how to speak, he stammered and pronounced the words wrong and repeated phrases."

"And what did they expect? The Demosthenes of the underworld? But one could understand some of what he said, I imagine."

"He said—there in front of everybody, because trials are public—he said it was all true, can you believe what poor taste, talking about things that are not only private, but illicit. He said he was in love with that girl and she with him and he didn't see why they couldn't love each other and he was going to stop being king and he was going to go away with her and walk naked and barefoot through the fields and eat fruit and drink water from the rivers, what a crazy idea. It must have been so unpleasant for the Lords to see the same king they had elected sniveling and drooling like a fussy child in front of the people he supposedly had to govern. How could it be that no one moved or said anything when the Lord of Lords got down from the throne and took off his shoes which were of an extremely fine leather with gold buckles, and took off the embroidered cloak and the crown and, wearing only in a tunic of white linen, walked over to the exit?"

"And no one did anything?"

"The Lords did something. The Lords reacted and gave the order to the police to seize him and they carried him back to the throne. But what a strange thing, no one obeyed and the Lord of Lords kept walking and left the courtroom and reached the gardens."

"But, Trafalgar? What was Trafalgar doing that he didn't take advantage of the chance to escape?"

"He didn't? Sweetie, it's as if you didn't know him well. As soon as the Lord of Lords started to talk and everyone was watching him, Medrano backed up and put himself out of the guards' reach and when the king left the room and some Warriors and the Lords yelled and ran out, he ran, too."

"Well done, I like it."

"But he didn't go very far."

"They caught him again?"

"No, luckily not. In the Palace gardens, where there were always a lot of people, there was a big stir when they saw him appear barefoot, wearing only his underclothes. And then, Medrano was able to see it all well, then a very young, very pretty woman embraced him, crying: it was the Scholar's wife, she of the guilty passions."

"Oh, Josefina, that's a phrase out of a serial novel."

"Is it that way or is it not? A married woman who has a love affair with a man who is not her husband is blameworthy, and don't tell me no because that I will not accept."

"We aren't going to fight over it, especially now when you leave me hanging with everyone in such a foul predicament. Did Trafalgar do anything besides watch?"

"Quite a bit, poor boy, he was very generous. Mistaken, but generous. The Lords and the Warriors and the Scholars—not the Priests, because none of them were there, they lead quieter lives, as is proper— tried to get to the Lord of Lords and that woman, but all the people of the other castes who were in the garden and those who came in from outside or came out of the Palace to see, without knowing very well why—because many of them hadn't been at the tribunal; just out of rebelliousness or resentment, I imagine—started to defend them. Of course, that turned into a plain of Agramante and there was a terrible fight. The Warriors and the Lords had weapons, but those of the inferior castes destroyed the gardens, such a shame, pulling out stones, taking iron from the benches, chunks of marble and crystal from the fountains, branches, railings from the gazebos, anything with which to attack and give the Lord of Lords and the woman time to escape."

"And did they escape?"

"They escaped. And your friend Medrano after them. He says his private plane, he doesn't call it private plane, what does he call it?"

"Clunker."

"That's it. He says his private plane wasn't very far away and he wanted to get to it, very sensible it seems to me, and take off immediately. But meanwhile the Lords and Warriors got organized, they called in soldiers, who I think are from the Warriors caste, too, but are doing their apprenticeship, and they chased the Lord of Lords and the woman. That was when Medrano caught up with them and dragged them with him to the airplane."

"Thank goodness. You were starting to scare me."

"Go ahead and get scared, now comes the worst."

"Oh, no, don't tell me more."

"Fine, I won't tell you more."

"No, yes, tell me."

"Which is it?"

"Josefina, no, I promise I wasn't serious."

"I know, and anyway I can't cut the story short now. They had almost reached the plane, with the Lords and Warriors and the Scholars and the soldiers chasing them and behind them all those from the inferior castes who were throwing stones but no longer tried to get close because the Warriors had killed several, they had almost reached it when the Lords realized where they were going and that they were about to escape and they gave the order to the soldiers to fire. They shot, and they killed the Lord of Lords."

I said nothing. Josefina observed that it was getting dark, and I went inside and turned on the garden lights.

"Medrano," said my Aunt Josefina, "saw that they had put a bullet through his head and he grabbed the woman and pulled her up into the plane. But she didn't want to go, now that the Lord of Lords was dead, and she fought so hard that she managed to free herself and she threw herself out of the plane. Medrano tried to follow her and take her up again, but the Warriors and the Lords were already upon him and they kept firing and he had to close the door. They killed her, too. It was a horrible death, Medrano said, but he didn't explain how and I didn't ask. He remained locked in, on the ground but ready to take off, and saw they weren't paying attention to him any longer. In the end, to them he was no more than a foreigner from whom they had bought jewels, who perhaps understood nothing of the country's customs and so had done things that were not right. They went away and left the bodies. Those of the inferior castes had to be obliged to retreat at bayonet point because they wanted to come close at all costs although they were no longer throwing stones or anything else. And that was when Medrano left the pearl necklace. When he saw that he was alone, he got down from the plane, at great risk, it seems to me, but he was very brave and it's very moving, he got down from the plane and he put the string of pearls on the woman, on what remained of her, he said. Afterward he climbed back up, locked himself in, washed his hands, lit a cigarette, and lifted off."

"How awful."

"Yes. So long as it's true," said my Aunt Josefina. "I don't know what to think. Might it not be nothing more than a fairy tale for an old lady all alone drinking her tea?"

"Trafalgar doesn't tell fairy tales. And you're not old, Josefina, come on."

End of the Interval

Mr. Chaos

"What do I know?" said Trafalgar. "I've been so many places, done so many things, I get confused. Ask Elvira, she has everything noted down."

"Josefina was here the other day," I said, "and we drank tea here in the garden and she sat in the same chair where you're sitting and she said you had told her about Serprabel."

"Don't talk about it. It makes me sick to remember what they did to that poor girl."

So he drank the coffee and, for a while, said nothing. And I asked no questions: one can hurry Trafalgar along, discreetly, in the middle of a story but never before a story begins because then he starts talking about any old thing, about tangos, let's say, or he starts to make fun of himself and his adventures with women or in business and he goes on with the coffee and suddenly he leaves and one realizes one has been left without knowing what one wanted to know.

"That coffee must be cold," he said.

"You've drunk three cups."

"Go on, heat up what's left, all right? And while you're at it, make a little more."

I left him alone for a while in the garden.

"But that was on the last trip," he told me when I returned with the coffee pot. "On the other hand, nothing happened on this trip."

"You lie like a moron."

"Seriously. I made a lot of stops, all of them very short and in places I already knew from before except for two, so everything went very well and very quickly."

"And in those two places you didn't know from before, what happened?"

"Nothing," he opened another pack of cigarettes. "That's how I like coffee, good and hot. Although it's a little weak; your husband doesn't complain?"

"Don't forget he had an ulcer and can't drink strong coffee."

"Poor Goro, how could he avoid having an ulcer after twenty-five years of marriage."

"Go on, you defend bachelorhood. Some day you're going to marry a harpy who sweet-talks you into it and you're going to end up with ulcers, sciatica, and hives. You didn't meet any candidates on this trip?"

"More or less as usual."

"And on those two worlds that you hadn't been to?"

"Nothing worthwhile. A very pretty little blonde, crazier than a goat, on Akimaréz, but I got rid of her as soon as I could."

"What's that about Akimaréz? I don't remembering hearing you mention it."

"I must have told you something, because I knew it existed and that one could buy graphite and kaolin there. Cheaply, both of them. It's quite pretty, no great wonder, but it's not bad. Very big, lots of water and seven continents like enormous islands in the middle of the oceans. The islands have water and vegetation only at the edges and that's where they've planted their cities, which you can tell Goro are the dream of any urban planner: small cities, low buildings, never more than three stories, with gardens; little traffic, none of your noise or smoke or odor. They like music, too. And in the middle of the islands, of the continents, the landscape is fantastic, black and white, dry, impossible to fertilize. But what do they care? They sell the black graphite and the white kaolin and feldspar and granite and I don't know what else and they're sitting pretty, strumming their lutes."

"Cushy life."

"Yes, but boring. They have a good time, but I'd had enough after two days. I made my purchases and I left."

"And the other one you didn't know?"

"Aleiçarga. Almost the complete opposite: little sea and lots of green. Two itty-bitty seas at the poles and another larger one close to the equator. It rains a lot, the rest is fertile ground, and the cities are disgusting."

"Big, dirty, with smoke and drugs and loudspeakers."

"Not so fast. Small cities because they, and they're not the only ones, seem to have figured out what we are just learning; very clean, without smoke, don't even think about drugs, and a few loudspeakers but they're not bothersome."

"Then they're quite nice. I don't know why you say they're disgusting."

"They are too well organized."

"So far as I know, that is not a defect."

"You, being Madam Organization; but when a whole city and all of the cities and everything is like an enormous and efficient company presided over by a narrow gauge logic where the effects always follow the causes and the causes march along single file and the dodo birds don't worry about anything nor are they surprised by anything and they slither along beside you faintly pleased, I—like any normal person—feel a great desire to kill someone or commit suicide."

"Thank you."

"Don't be offended," he smiled at me a little. "On Akimaréz one gets bored but on Aleiçarga one has to be very careful so as not to fall into the trap and not to enter into the little game of being sensible. That's what it is, they are sensible, so much so that either they infect you or you do something awful."

"And what awful thing did you do?"

"Nothing. Didn't I tell you nothing happened?"

"Nothing, nothing at all?"

"Nothing, are you ever stubborn. I did the same as always: sell, talk, eat, sleep, walk around to get to know the place a bit. And I discovered an interesting guy. I think the coffee is running out."

"I'll make you more if you tell me who the guy was and why he was interesting."

"I don't know who he was, I never learned his name. And he was interesting because he wasn't sensible."

"No?"

"No. He was crazy. And if there's no more coffee, I'm leaving."

"Blackmailer."

"You started."

I went to make the coffee and I thought it was a sure thing that Trafalgar had been lying when he said nothing had happened and he had done nothing.

"And?" I asked him from the kitchen doorway.

"And what?"

"And the crazy guy?"

"Look, there are so many crazies around, who cares about one more?"

"I care. Here comes the coffee."

A hassle with the coffeepot. If I took it good and full, it would get cold; if I only took a little, I would have to make more. But as with Trafalgar one has to learn to resign oneself to the coffee, I took it half full.

"Let's go, tell me."

"But *che*, I already told you there's nothing to tell. The Aleiçarganos are sensible, rational, efficient, measured, discreet, and this other one was just the opposite, so he was listed as crazy."

"But listen, one can be just the opposite of efficient and discreet and sensible and not be crazy. Are you sure he was crazy?"

"No."

"Ah-ha."

"Have we begun?"

"We haven't started anything," I watched him swallow the coffee. "Couldn't you be more or less efficient and sensible and for once start at the beginning?"

"Ugh, all right, I arrived on Aleiçarga on a spring day at nine fifteen in the morning, I got out, locked the clunker, went to the reception office, I was received very well by a short little guy and another fellow, a little taller and very fat, the port wasn't very big but it was very complete, they gave me coffee, they arranged all the paperwork in a flash—it wasn't much—they pointed me to a hotel and I went there, using very comfortable public transport, at the hotel I had breakfast and more coffee."

"I am going to strangle you."

"I went up to my room, I bathed, I changed, I didn't shave because I had shaved prior to arrival, I left the hotel, took a taxi, went to the Center of Commerce, spoke to the secretary, a birdlike man who resembled a tero, I inquired whether they were interested in buying kaolin and graphite, he said yes, we went to lunch together."

"Go. Out of my house. I don't want to see you again in my life."

"Wait, wait a little. At the beginning I thought everything was perfect and I didn't like that because you know perfect things smell bad to me; if I have to choose a glass from Murano, I choose one that has a bubble. But as besides rolling along smoothly, everything benefited me, I let myself be fooled—sweet-talked, as you say. Hey, where's the cat? I don't see her."

"She went out for a drink with the tomcat next door. Go on."

"Of course, I'm not a total moron and it didn't take long for me to wise up."

"I would like Josefina to have heard that phrase."

"Because?"

"Nothing. Go on."

"One's used to the word perfect and we use it when something went well, end of story. But if something is perfect perfect, without fissures or mending, then it is very bad," he smoked and drank coffee and maybe looked around for the cat. "Anything heavenly is necessarily hellish."

And another threat of violent ejection must have floated in the air because he hurried on:

"On Aleiçarga, everyone has a placid face and smiles once in a while but no one guffaws, no one yells, no one runs to catch the bus and if they catch it they don't fight with the driver and if they don't catch it they don't swear, no kid comes to blows with another or cries, begging for gum with trading cards." He set the empty cup on the saucer. "Gum probably doesn't come with trading cards."

And he served himself more coffee and I waited because by now it seemed unlikely that he would cut short the story about how nothing, but absolutely nothing, had happened.

"I don't know for certain," he said, "because I'm not among the idiots who chew gum. In the evening I returned to the Center with the secretary; the possible buyers were already there. I asked for quite a bit. Well, I'll tell you I asked for a lot, a matter of then coming down a bit. They smiled, they said no and they stood up to leave. I stood there with my mouth open. It was just unbelievable: they didn't know how to haggle."

"So what? I imagine there are people who don't haggle."

"I'm not saying there aren't. But few, believe me, very few. Almost none. Some more, some less, but everybody argues over prices. And there are places where bargaining is a refined art, sublime, places where you have to go very well prepared, otherwise you're toast. I am no master but I do have some experience. And there, with the guys about to get away from me, it occurred to me that I could invent a story for them and say I came from a place where bargaining is a form of commercial courtesy and give them the whole song and dance, but I realized the best thing to do would be to grab the bull by the horns and before they finished saying good-bye I showed them my cards. They were a little disoriented but they understood right away. Everyone understands everything right away on that lousy world. No, don't take it away, it's still drinkable. I sold everything I had in half a minute."

"Don't tell me at a ridiculously low price, because I won't believe you."

"Ridiculously low, no; sensible, that's the problem, sensible, reasonable. It's not that I didn't earn anything, no, that's not allowed on Aleiçarga precisely because it's not reasonable or logical. I made a profit, but not so much as if they had let me hold forth like a silver-tongued huckster in the bazaar. And they took care of everything, the invoices, the permits, the seals, the unloading, everything. So one minute later I had nothing more to do and the next day I could leave."

"And why didn't you leave? Tell me that."

"How do you know I didn't leave?"

"The crazy guy, dear, I'm waiting for the crazy guy to appear."

"I didn't leave because I was ticked at them. I thought up a few dirty tricks, like for example mixing lower quality kaolin with the first-class stuff, cheating them on the weight, getting myself invited to the guys' homes and seducing their wives and daughters."

"Don't puff yourself up."

"I'm not puffing myself up. I was playing with my irritation, that's all. And they weren't so many. With a little time, who can say?"

And he smiled again, not at me but at the hypothetical daughters of the kaolin buyers.

"Instead of that. Understand me, I didn't mix the merchandise nor did I fix the weight, because a person has scruples. Sometimes. And I didn't try to meet the daughters because surely if the fathers don't know how to haggle, the girls don't know how to flirt before saying yes."

"Or no. Instead of that, what did you do?"

"Or no, you're right. Instead of that, I asked the secretary where there was a bookstore."

"A bookstore."

"Not on a whim. When you go to a place of which you know nothing and no one, you have to seek out three things: bookstores, temples, and brothels. There are others, of course, in case you don't find any of the former: you can also go to the schools, the casinos, the hospitals, the barracks. But I had seen bookstores and I opted for the safe choice. I told the guy I wanted to buy something to read that night in the hotel and he sent me to a little bookstore that had everything, understand?"

"I don't know what I'm supposed to understand, don't make yourself mysterious."

"That little is written on Aleiçarga, very little. A single monumental work of history with its corresponding compendium in one volume, laws, mathematics, medicine, physics, logic, not more than half a dozen novels, no poetry."

"What brutes."

"That's what you think. And when you go to the bookstore, you have to buy two things: history and a novel. I bought the compendium and a novel called *The Ragemca.*"

"The what did you say?"

"It's a surname. It was the story of a family. And I read both of them that same night and I almost died of boredom. I read the history first and I learned that nothing had ever happened. It is assumed that the first Aleiçarganos lived in the forests, naked, eating fruit and sleeping under the climbing vines, all very healthy. And that they had wooden instruments and when they died they weren't buried but rather raised up to the highest branches and tied up there, probably to save them a leg of the journey, but that's what I say, not the historians of Aleiçarga who don't permit themselves such fantasies. Later they built houses out of wood, of course, and they planted, made fire, the wheel arrived and after that the alphabet and that's it, the end."

"That's it how? They wrote a whole history book for that stupid little story?"

"That was the most interesting part. When they invented writing, and you can see the prehistoric ones walking around under the trees were more interesting than the modern folk if they thought up the wheel and the alphabet, with writing they started making chronicles of what happened, but the problem is nothing happened. According to the first writings, no one stole fire from the gods, the spirits of the forest never spoke to the people, perhaps because there were no spirits of the forest, the dead died and bye-bye, there was no hero who got lost searching for immortality, no woman cuckolded her husband with a demigod, and so on. So what remained was deadly dull: the harvests, the journeys, the plagues, a casual discovery or two, and nothing more."

"Legends?" I asked. "Sagas? Cosmogonies? Mythologies? Dreams?"

"The Aleiçarganos? Come on, it's so obvious you don't know them. With the wheel, fire, writing, a little bit of empirical medicine, another bit of engineering and architecture, also empirical, and no birth control or natural catastrophes or dangerous animals, they expanded and from the beginning they had a single state, a single government, plenty of work, no religion or poetry or politics."

"Wars," I thought. "There will have been wars, invasions, dethroned kings, junior officers with imperial ambitions, assassinations for power, don't tell me no."

"I'm telling you no. Those who are most fit to govern, govern. Those who are most fit to operate are surgeons. Those who are most fit to drive a tractor."

"Drive a tractor, thank you, I get it. But then without visionaries, without ambitions or schemers or prophets or delusionals, can you tell me how they moved forward?"

"Very slowly. They are very old and they had a lot of time."

"They're a bunch of dim bulbs."

"Agreed. The most spectacular, the great inventions, what they set aside because they thought it was impossible, all that came to them from outside. They still had wooden plows and carts pulled by oxen tied at the neck and wood stoves when other people who already traveled among the stars reached them and taught them things. Then they started to advance for real, because they learn quickly, so long as the big ideas occur to others."

"I don't see how they didn't just keep swinging from the trees. Tell me, and the novel?"

"Even more boring than the history text. Generations and generations of a family of industrious idiots, in which there were neither fights nor adultery nor fraudulent bankruptcies nor clashes between father and son; nor crazy aunts nor incest nor monsters nor geniuses, nothing, nothing, nothing. I fell asleep when I don't know which son of I don't know who and married to I don't know who else was building a house I don't know where and opening a factory of I don't know what and had three sons and a daughter."

"The next time, don't sell them graphite, sell them the complete works of Shakespeare and Balzac and you'll kill them all with a heart attack."

"Not even that. To start, I'm not going back. And if I go and I sell them Shakespeare and Balzac, I'll bet whatever you like that they read them, study them, and decide it's all a bunch of nonsense."

"I congratulate you. What an enjoyable trip."

"I told you and you didn't believe me."

"Because a person knows you already."

I almost stood up to go make more coffee but I remembered something and started to doubt again.

"Wait a sec. The crazy guy?"

"Well, of course, the crazy. Yes, the crazy. I met him the next day, at night. I couldn't bring myself to leave and I was still wandering around there. I couldn't believe, being used to, as you know, so many strange and absurd and stupid things not only here but on many other worlds, I couldn't believe there existed people who were so reasonable, but I was becoming convinced and I was almost taken over by so much calm. I went for a walk, I left the city and followed the walking paths that run beside the roads and that from time to time open and take you to the fields or the forests. The guy was sitting on the ground, whistling. When I heard the whistle I thought, no, it can't be. They don't have poets, did I tell you? Or musicians, except for dancing at parties or accompanying physical activities. For that matter, no painters, either. Illustrators, yes, but no painters. So nobody whistles, doesn't that seem reasonable to you? What for? No, of course, why would they whistle? And I was hearing a whistle, a little monotonous but the whistle of a person whistling because they feel like it, how's that? I stopped short and asked myself if I might not be the one whistling. No, it wasn't me. I left the path, set off toward the forest, and I found him."

He was quiet. And the worst of it was, he didn't even demand coffee.

"Trafalgar," I said.

"Huh?"

"I imagine you're not going to leave me hanging there."

"No."

"I'll make you coffee."

"Fine."

I went, heated the water, made coffee, returned, Trafalgar served himself and drank half the cup.

"He was huge," he said, "and blond and he had a beard and he whistled, seated on the ground. I said hello, good evening, and he answered that the cranes."

"That the cranes what?"

"Nothing, that's it, that the cranes."

He drank the other half of the cup and served himself more.

"Right then, and note that I am not sentimental."

"I don't know."

"I'm not. Right then I remembered a stupid game my cousins and I played when we were kids at the estate in Moreno and I came to the realization that it wasn't a stupid game. Someone said a sentence and the others had to answer in turn, quickly, with sentences that had nothing to do with the previous ones. It seems easy until you try. You can't think of anything beforehand, because you don't know what those who go before you are going to say, so suddenly you have to say something and if you take too long or if what you say is related to what has already been said, you blew it. There were more times we had to pay a forfeit than that we got it right. Hello, good evening and immediately: that the cranes, sounded like that. Look, there's the cat."

"I'm going to turn on the light."

"There you have it. We just did the same thing. There's the cat, I'm going to turn on the light. Is it reasonable or not?"

"No, but we understand each other, so it's fine."

"We don't understand each other, we comprehend each other and of course it's fine. But the Aleiçarganos didn't share that opinion and said the guy was crazy."

I went to turn on the light and when I returned Trafalgar was serving himself more coffee.

"We had a very interesting conversation. I still didn't know who he was nor what he was, but starting from the cranes and what I remembered from Moreno, I went forward. If I'd been playing with my cousins I'd have had to pay the forfeit because I was quiet for a

145

while thinking about everything I told you before, but I laughed to myself, I forgot I was on Aleiçarga and I said, you know what?"

He didn't expect me to answer, nor did he give me time to say no, how was I going to know?

"My cousin Alicia is married to a Japanese."

In fact, poor Alicia Salles, who is very pretty but quite silly, is married to a nice, bald dermatologist from Salta.

"And then, magnificently, he answered that there was a lot to say about paper flowers so long as they were pink. And I told him my wristwatch was five minutes fast. Or slow, I don't remember."

"I don't understand how you remember so many unconnected things."

"I remember perfectly because they're not unconnected."

"Come on, old man, hello, the cranes, the watch, the retard Alicia, the paper flowers, the imaginary Japanese—come on."

"And?"

"And what?"

"Are you going to tell me my watch has never been five minutes slow and my cousin Alicia isn't married and you don't have paper flowers on that coat stand and there is no Japanese married to a woman named Alicia and there aren't cranes somewhere?"

I wanted to protest but he didn't let me.

"More than that. Are you going to tell me that at some moment a Japanese—just as much as Alicia and you and I and the crazy—hasn't seen cranes or thought about cranes or about pink paper flowers and Alicia hasn't had a wristwatch that ran fast and some crane won't have flown by—well, I don't know if cranes fly like storks or if they walk around pecking at worms like chickens—flown by over a tower that had a clock that ran fast and over a store where they sold paper flowers?"

"Yes, I get it," I said.

And I got it. There in the dark garden everything was one great fresco moving with the wild and strict ballet of the cranes and the watches and the Alicias and the Japanese and the paper flowers and more, many more things and people and animals and plants and

Trafalgar and I and the cat, the cats, the book covers, necklaces, salt, warriors, eyeglasses, hats, old photographs, chandeliers and trains, Giorgio Morandi's bottles, gray moths, streetcar tickets, quill pens, emperors and sleeping pills, axes, incense and chocolate. And even more. Everything, to tell the truth.

Then Alicia isn't a retard.

"Your cousin Alicia isn't a retard," I said, "at least no more than anyone else. Why don't we always talk, all of us, like you and your cousins in Moreno or like the crazy guy on Aleiçarga?"

"Because we're afraid, I think," said Trafalgar. "And he wasn't crazy, it was that Aleiçarga had finally acquired, like no other world in the universe—in the one I know—the true awareness of total order. For the moment all they can do is reject it, of course, that's why they say he's crazy, but I don't think that will last long."

As we were also spinning comfortably in the universe, in the one we know for now, we had forgotten about the coffee not because we were thinking about other things but because we were also aware of all of the coffee possible and it was there and I could make more at that moment or three hours or ten months or seven years later because time was there, too.

"In other places," Trafalgar said, smoking, "right here, that awareness is fragmented and hidden. You would have to put together, for example, I don't know, a goatherd, a mathematician, a sage, a child who doesn't yet go to school, a schizophrenic, a woman giving birth, a teacher, a person dying, an I don't know what, I don't know how many more, and it could be that you would approach from a distance the true panorama. There they had everything in just two halves. On one side the sensible, logical, rational, efficient Aleiçarganos, incapable of a paradox, a vice, a sonata, an absurd joke, a haiku. And on the other, the crazy."

"He wasn't crazy."

"No, of course he wasn't crazy. They said he was because if they accepted him, it shook everything up for them. But I decided he wasn't crazy. He was."

"I'm going to make you more coffee," I said.

"Go on."

And he got up and went into the kitchen with me.

"He was primordial chaos," he said while the water heated and I washed the coffee pot. "He saw the forms and so what he said seemed unformed; he lived all times and so he spoke without order; he was so complete that one couldn't span him fully but saw him fragmented, and so normal that the Aleiçarganos said he was crazy. I think he was what we should have already become."

Trafalgar picked up the coffee pot and we went back to the garden where the cat was lying in wait for gray moths that had come to the light. He drank a cup of coffee and took out cigarettes and he offered them to me but I don't smoke the black ones.

"I don't know how you can smoke that trash," he said. "It rusts your lungs."

"Oh, of course, the black ones don't."

"They do, too, but less." He served himself more coffee.

"Was it the only time you saw him?"

"Who?"

"Him. Mr. Chaos."

"Uh-huh. But so what? I saw him one time, two, twenty, a million times. And I was with him until dawn. An entire night talking and talking without stopping and without paying a forfeit for anything because we couldn't be mistaken, ever; I went back to the hotel when the sun was high but as fresh as if I had slept for ten hours."

"You came back that day?"

"That night. In the morning I looked for the secretary of the Center of Commerce and asked him directly who he was. The guy smiled. He smiled discreetly, with a smile so reasonable, so without indulgence, without embarrassment, without malice, without anything, so much a smile and nothing more than a smile, that I don't know how I managed not to grab him by the suit and shake him until his brains were scrambled. He told me he was an unfortunate who had been born that way and he even explained why but I preferred to draw the curtain and I didn't hear that part. He told me they had tried to cure him but without success and I thought, what luck, and he told me, this will kill you, that they had thought about eliminating him but that as he was harmless, they allowed him to live and the municipality was responsible for feeding and clothing him. And as I kept asking, he told me he lived in a house the municipality loaned him and they also paid people to keep it in reasonable condition. And that he, the crazy, at the beginning gave them a lot to do because every morning the house was disarranged, with the furniture in the patio or the mattress in the bathtub or the rug on the roof or the frying pans hanging from the latch or things like that until they had nailed everything, not the frying pans, to the floor or the walls and since then the guy went there seldom and preferred to live in the forest like the savages, that's what he said, like the savages."

"The savages."

"Yes, but don't think about Thoreau, think about the savages."

"Of course."

"But he told me something more."

And he was quiet. I served him coffee and I waited for him; I waited for a long time.

"He told me they were thinking about reconsidering the benevolent attitude. Because it seemed that in his way Mr. Chaos had started courting the girls."

"Those who didn't know how to flirt before they said yes. The daughters of those who didn't know how to bargain."

"The same. I trust one of them will learn," said Trafalgar, "before the Aleiçarganos have time to reconsider anything. What I rely on is that, as is the case everywhere, the women on Aleiçarga will be more curious, more audacious, wiser than the men; like mother Eve, they will quickly eat the apple while that wimpy Adam waffles. I don't dare hope it will be many of them but one, one at least, I am confident that one will say yes."

"And if they kill him?"

"It could be that they kill him. But I think that is no longer important."

The cat was getting impatient.

"It must be late," Trafalgar said.

"That's not important either," I answered. "I'm going to feed the cat."

"It seems to me," I heard him say from the kitchen, "that she tired of the gray moths and the pink paper flowers."

Constancia

"I can't," Jorge said, "I have to leave right away."

Trafalgar let Marcos know he wanted another coffee.

"Fine," he said, "but at least have a cup of coffee."

"I won't say no to that," and out came one of those pipes he talks about so much.

"What do you have in that briefcase? Luggage?"

"Books, what do you expect me to carry? Books are my good luck and my misfortune."

"Who do you sell them to, with that beat-up bag?"

"There are always customers. Sentimental spinsters getting on in years (the others don't waste their time reading), who buy happy endings in sad novels, or first-time parents, a sure bet for encyclopedias."

"May those specimens never die out on you. It has happened that I have found myself without any customers, not one. Do you know how depressing it is to arrive at a place and there's no one there?"

"No, I don't know, and I hope not to find out, thank you."

"Then don't ever go to Donteä-Doreä."

"What a name, what a mouthful of a name."

"Yes," said Trafalgar, "for a poem, but not for one of yours."

"Hold it right there. Leave me with Los Quirquinchos which, as a name, sounds much better."

"Donteä-Doreä is for heroes lost after a battle and ready to be dumped on by destiny. If it's possible, at the edge of the cliffs and with the roaring sea there below."

"And the mists," Jorge pitched in, "don't forget the mists, which are important, nor the disheveled blondes who have premonitions in far off lands."

"Let's not continue. I don't think there are cliffs on Donteä-Doreä. And she wasn't blonde, she was a striking brunette."

"Ah," said Jorge and he took a draw on his pipe and then remembered. "But wasn't there nobody there?"

"The thing is, it's a little complicated." Trafalgar drank some coffee, smoked, considered the situation and studied those assembled in the Burgundy. "Are you going to leave with books and everything, or will you stay and listen to me?"

"I'll stay, but only if you tell me quickly, let's say in five minutes."

"Bye-bye," said Trafalgar.

"What's this bye-bye?"

"Do you write a poem, let's say, in five minutes?"

Jorge laughed, cleaned his pipe, put it away and took out another. Trafalgar doesn't get the pipe thing.

"I don't get the pipe thing," Trafalgar said. "All that work, for what?"

"I'll stay but let's not digress," Jorge prodded him.

Marcos came over, left the coffee, heard that about digressions and went away, smiling at Jorge.

"Donteä-Doreä," said Trafalgar. "The problem is there is a lot of wind, but it's not ugly. I ended up there by chance," he drank coffee and lit a black, unfiltered cigarette while Jorge used the twenty-second match on the second pipe. "I was coming from Yereb which is a world you would like a lot. All fertile soil and rivers. Populated by hardworking, hard-drinking, troublemaking farmers. Montagues and Capulets, hereditary enemies, they fight over a woman, over a piece of land, over a pick and a spade, over anything, and afterward they make up at big open-air banquets where two or three more fights are sure to break out."

"What did you sell them? Boxing gloves?"

"Electrical appliances for the home."

"Are you kidding me?"

"Didn't I tell you they're farmers? They export grains, flours, wood, natural fertilizers, fibers, all that, and they import what the surrounding worlds manufacture and on top of that they earn money and live like nobles in huge farmhouses with high ceilings and thick walls and Olympic patios."

"Not bad."

"Like hell, it's not bad. You tell me; there's a lot of work, otherwise it would be worth going to live on Yereb. And there they saddled me with a passenger."

"I thought you never took anyone along when you traveled."

"Uh-huh. That's my preference. But I'm not inflexible. In a few cases I'm willing to make exceptions and the boy struck me as a nice guy. He was a mechanic from Sebdoepp. Mechanics from Sebdoepp are serious business. It's a horrible world, full of electrical storms, one after the other, day and night, an unlivable place where you never see the sun and where you have to go out in the open with an anchor because the wind drags you away. As the inhabitants weren't inclined to emigrate—I don't know why, because you have to be crazy to want to live there—they started moving into caves, they kept digging tunnels from cave to cave and they ended up living in fabulous cities built underground."

"Get out of there. I'm dying, it gives me claustrophobia."

"Don't talk until you've seen the cities of Sebdoepp."

"Frankly, don't count on me, leave me in Rosario where on Sunday mornings I can go play soccer in Urquiza Park with the boys."

"In the cities of Sebdoepp you can also go to the field to play soccer, better put to play pekidep which is a lot more fun although with a higher risk of breaking one or more bones. There's an artificial sun, and moon, natural rivers, forests—half natural, half artificial— dawns, middays, afternoons, and nights (also artificial), natural lakes, it's fantastic."

"Do you want to come to Urquiza Park on Sunday?"

"I don't play soccer and I warn you I don't play pekidep either, but if it's nice out, I'll go. You can imagine that to have done all that and maintained it in functioning conditions and then answer to millions of inhabitants, you have to be very skilled. There isn't a man or woman on Sebdoepp who isn't an artist when it comes to engineering, physics, chemistry, mechanics. All of the worlds recognize the mechanics from Sebdoepp, and there was one on Yereb, installing I don't know what devices to improve the performance of the agricultural machines, and I took him with me."

"To the place with the disheveled blonde who was really a striking brunette?"

"Ah, yes," Trafalgar sighed. "Hey, where's Marcos?"

The Burgundy was almost full but Trafalgar didn't manage to turn all the way around looking for him, because Marcos was already there with the coffee.

"To Donteä-Doreä," he said, "where we weren't, in fact, going."

"Huh?"

"No, we weren't going there. I didn't even have it registered. We were going to Sebdoepp from where the Yerebianos had brought that young guy, Side Etione-Dól was his name, and where instead of taking him back themselves, they proposed I should take him, since I was going that way, beyond Sebdoepp, to buy Ksadollamis pearls. I said yes and we set out, but not even halfway through the trip, we discovered we had to land somewhere, anywhere, because something had come loose, not in the clunker's motor, because the clunker's motor never fails, but on the outside. And we landed on Donteä-Doreä, which is uninhabited."

"And the brunette?"

"Wait, don't rush me. As I was telling you, there's wind there, a lot of wind, and a pile of ruins. Rich and powerful people must have lived on Donteä-Doreä, but so long ago that there's nothing left but stones. We landed and Side—a tall, tousled blond, nice guy—who plays the harmonica and whistles, it's a pleasure to hear him, grabbed a pair of pliers, a couple of wires, and a special cement they use, and in two seconds, he had fixed what was broken."

Trafalgar was quiet, as if he were listening to the conversations in the Burgundy, and Jorge smoked his pipe and waited; he waited a good while.

"And afterward, curiosity did us in," said Trafalgar.

"And you met the brunette."

"Tell me, are you obsessed with brunettes?"

"And blondes. And all of them. Admit, there's nothing nicer than women."

"Hmmmmm," went Trafalgar.

They probably thought about whether there was anything nicer than women, although what conclusion they reached is unknown, while Marcos gave them a quick look in passing, a matter of finding out if he needed to bring them more coffee.

"It happened that we had landed close to a city, a city in ruins, of course. And as the clunker was all ready five minutes after we landed, and as there was a wind that for Side was a light spring breeze although to me it was the furious sirocco, and as we had nothing to do, we put our hands in our pockets and started to walk toward the city, which must have been immense. Under the wind and against the light like that, it looked as if it had been carved out in huge bites. When we reached the outer walls, we looked at each other as if to say, now what do we do? And what we did was pick a street and head toward the center."

"It would be a little bigger than Rosario, I imagine."

"Easily, easily, a city for ten million inhabitants. And not a bit of brick or cement: stone, all stone. Big, carved stones, sometimes colored and with the round edges made to fit one into another so they'd never move again. Mycenae. A Mycenae the size of Greater Buenos Aires. A lot was still standing and a lot was spilled over the streets, which were double and triple as wide as one of our avenues, and in the plazas which, from their size, could have served as soccer fields. And there we were walking, Side and I, like a couple hicks looking at everything, he whistling and me fighting the wind that was boxed in between the partial walls."

Jorge settled himself more comfortably in the chair and picked up the pipe, which had gone out a good while ago, put it in his mouth and chewed on it slowly, thinking about ruins in the rain, perhaps.

"We were well inside by then," said Trafalgar, "where the city was less ruined, more impressive, and lonelier. And suddenly something moved on the second floor of a building that had the look of a ministry or temple or something like that. Marcos, do you believe in destiny?"

"Me?" said Marcos. He set two coffees on the table. "Don't give me a hard time. I'll bring you cold water. But on Sunday there's a race-horse registered in the fourth race named My Destiny and a real loser is riding him. I'm going to put a few pesos on it."

"There you have it," said Trafalgar when Marcos was leaving.

"There you have what?" Jorge wanted to know. The question came out a little garbled because he was still chewing on that famous pipe.

"Side said it had been the work of destiny after all, and I said the only destiny that exists is each person's stupidity."

"Good, that's fine, but what was it that moved on the second floor of the ministry?"

"We never knew if it had been a ministry or a temple. Side knows a lot about mechanics, a lot. But not all of the places I travel through are peaceful and delightful like Eiquen or Akimaréz. There are some in which you have to be well prepared for anything and have quick reflexes or you don't come back again. Up to now, my reflexes are in good shape. We hadn't seen animals or birds or any living thing, so as soon as I saw movement, I threw myself against Side and the two of us tumbled to the ground. Thank goodness, because the shots started immediately."

"Shots?" Jorge took the pipe out of his mouth and set it on the table.

"Shots. From a shotgun. We crawled over behind a huge rock that had fallen at the edge of the plaza. We heard another couple of shots and then nothing. I took off my jacket, rolled it up in a ball and raised it over the edge of the rock. Whoever was shooting was shoot-ing to kill: it was shot full of holes."

"Shit."

"I said something similar, though at greater length."

"And what did you do?"

"When a city is in ruins, it's uncomfortable to live in but it has other advantages for less peaceful activities. Crawling along, we got into the house closest to us, and as they were all gutted, we passed from one to another through holes in the walls or wherever we found an opening, circling the plaza and getting close to the building the shots had come from. During all of this the shooter was quiet, either thinking we'd been hit or waiting to see what we did."

"And how did you know there was only one shooter?"

"That question occurred to us on the way and we sat down on some stone benches—I said they were from a waiting room and Side said a school—to consider the possibilities. If there had been two, the shooting would have been heavier. And if there had been more than two, they wouldn't even have let us get that far, since being on a war footing, they'd have posted sentinels. So there was only one. Or two but with only one weapon. And as we were developing a strong desire to land a good slug or two, we went on."

Trafalgar pushed the cup away and leaned over the table: "We surprised him from behind," he said, "after we climbed a staircase in quite good condition, barefoot so our shoes wouldn't make noise against the stones. The guy had his back to us, looking out, close against the edge of the window, with the shotgun stock down on the ground. The blondie with the harmonica and I looked at each other, we made a sign and we jumped at the same moment: I went for the shotgun and he for the shooter. And when I stood up with the weapon in my hand, this will kill you, I hear him give out a yell."

"The guy?"

"Side. Are you going to have more coffee?"

"No, that's enough for me. And why did he yell?"

"Because it wasn't a guy, it was a girl."

"The brunette."

"That's it, the brunette. Of course, poor Side had grabbed her from behind to immobilize her arms and when he squeezed and got such a surprise, he yelled and let go, the big idiot."

"Myself, not just to talk, but if that happened to me, I wouldn't let anything go, I'd hold tight like a bear's claw."

"It's that Side's a romantic."

"As am I."

157

"You, too, would have let her go."

Jorge laughed. "I don't know, eh? I don't know."

"Ha," said Trafalgar. "The brunette slipped through our fingers and tried to escape. She knew the territory but we were two and in the end we had the pleasure of catching her. Well, miss, I said, very formal but with the voice of a monitor who's caught a student smoking in the bathroom, what's all this going around shooting at people? All right, she said, you win, take me but I warn you, I won't arrive alive."

By this point in the story there weren't many people left in the Burgundy and, according to Trafalgar, on Donteä-Doreä, night was falling.

"We told her we didn't intend to take her anywhere and that we had landed there by chance and we made her promise she wouldn't try to kill us or to escape and we let go of her. And she didn't try to escape or to kill us. She straightened her clothes, she was dressed all in black and she had a silver necklace, she straightened her clothes, she fixed the bun that had started to come undone, and she started to bustle around the room, which was very large and in good condition. She covered the windows with shutters, lit the lamps, straightened up the mess we had made a bit, and invited us to sit down."

"Where did you sit, on the ground?"

"What ground, she had installed a real little palace there. The lamps and the heaters had solar batteries that were practically eternal, the stove too. The floor was covered with rugs and there was furniture and clothing and dishes and knickknacks and books and recorded tapes. The table was carved out of a single piece of wood from Neyiomdav by a cabinetmaker who knew what he was doing, and the chairs matched and had feather cushions. On the floor, all along the walls decorated with tapestries and pictures, there were more feather cushions and what must have been a queen-sized bed, at least, with a fur blanket in black and white."

"Sensational," Jorge said. "Let's see if you'll act like a friend and give me that girl's address."

"Sadly," said Trafalgar, "Side got there ahead of you. Besides, your wife would strangle you, so give it up."

"Don't tell me the blond picked her up."

"He may have believed in destiny, but he was no idiot. We sat down and we asked each other who we were and we told about ourselves. Side told her, and when I saw how he exaggerated everything, the breakdown, his skill, my importance, I thought, we're toast, romance at the door. And I kept quiet and watched her and there was something about her that caught my attention."

"How was she, just between us?"

"A babe. Tall, with hair that was blue, it was so black and shiny; no makeup, skin like a gypsy's, almond-shaped eyes, high cheekbones, roman nose, very white teeth, a strong chin and everything else to stop traffic."

"How was she not going to catch your attention?"

"No, what caught my attention was her attitude," said Trafalgar, and he devoted himself to his coffee.

"Cut it out, what attitude? Come on."

"Kind but condescending, haughty, as if giving us permission, do you see? How can I put it—Pharaonic, that's it, Pharaonic."

"You were dreaming about Nefertiti."

"Exactly. Nefertiti. So long as Nefertiti looked like a model for *Vogue.*"

"No wonder the blond was showing off."

"Yes, he kept talking for half an hour or so. And she was very quiet, looking at him, which you can imagine only made things worse. When the poor thing finished, he looked like a Spanish water dog."

"And you?"

"I asked her, and who are you, miss? My name is Constancia, she said. It's a beautiful name, said that idiot Side. As this threatened to turn into a television soap opera, I asked why she had received us with shotgun fire and instead of answering me she said yes, it was a very pretty name but it reminded her of her world where every woman of her class bore the name of a virtue. I insisted and she asked if we wanted to eat something and Side answered yes for both of us. That suited me, because it was already late at night and I was starting to miss the provisions in the clunker. And I remembered the clunker and

I said we had to go back but she said there was no danger because on Donteä-Doreä there was absolutely no one but her. And she proposed that we spend the night there and Side practically dies from excitement and goes and says yes, of course, why not, certainly, with pleasure, ugh."

"Well, you could have gone alone."

"Forget it. She said there was no one besides her on Donteä-Doreä but although I thought she was telling the truth, she could well have been lying. And so long as I stayed, I would be able to keep an eye on her, leaving aside the fact that I wanted to find out who she was, what had happened to her, why she was so afraid that she met people with shotgun fire. Bah, so we stayed. Don't make that face, she slept all alone in the big bed and we made ourselves another bed with the cushions that were enough for a battalion. But first we ate, and very well. With those airs of a duchess, I thought she was going to give us a couple of fried eggs with the yolk hard and the white raw and stuck to the pan, but she managed a kind of *soufflé aux fines herbes* that left us licking our fingers. And for dessert, fruit with cream. And a very good wine, and coffee, nearly perfect coffee."

"Nearly."

"Nearly. She had put sugar in it. But I drank it anyway. Three cups. After that I couldn't stand any more and I asked her for a fourth cup without sugar."

"But listen, where did she get the things to cook if there were no plants or animals or anything?"

"She had a pantry on the ground floor in a kind of auditorium. Full, so full that not even living there for more than a century would she manage to eat it all, and with a freezer system that made even Side whistle when he saw it, and not exactly a song, either."

"Yes, yes, but where had she gotten ahold of all that?"

"You'll see. After dinner, Side took out his harmonica and started playing syrupy ballads that would melt glaciers and she remained quiet and watched him and now and then smiled at him and nodded approval. It you asked the poor guy at that moment to change the washer in the faucet, he'd make a complete hash of it. Until I stood up, took away the harmonica, and said to her, well Constancia, now tell us something about yourself. She looked at me as though I were made of glass and behind me were something that bored her to tears. So I said to her, you are from Sondarbedo IV, isn't that right?"

"And how did you know?"

"I didn't know, how would I know? Anyway, Sondarbedo IV doesn't exist. She said no. Nothing more than no. She didn't say no, I am from such and such a place. And Side, who was floating half a meter off the ground, resolved the situation by force of artlessness. He told her we wanted to help her. I didn't have the least little intention of helping her, because, although I liked the girl, I also distrusted her. But I kept quiet to see what happened. And he told her we were going to do whatever was necessary so that she wouldn't continue to live like that, alone and cornered. Side was inspired. And then she cried."

"When a woman pulls the tears ploy on you, old man, she has won the battle."

"No, I'm not sure it was a ploy. She didn't need tears—what for, if she already had Side in her pocket? The tears welled up on their own, and Side knighted himself and would have straight away started fighting the suicidal archers of Ssouraa."

"Who?"

"In reality, the suicidal archers of Ssouraa live on Aloska VI, because on account of wars, there's nothing left on Ssouraa. They're suicidal battalions that use atomic weapons that resemble bows and that."

"No, enough, you can tell me that another day. Now what I want to know is what happened with Constancia."

"She softened and started to tell everything. I'll summarize for you, because the explanation was too long and too mushy for my taste. Constancia had been lady-in-waiting to the queen on Adrojanmarain, very far from Donteä-Doreä, a world with very advanced technology and very backward morality. These contradictions occur sometimes, but once you study them in depth, you see they're not really contradictions. Look at Na-man III, for example, where they haven't reached the steam engine yet but where . . ."

"Do me a favor, don't tell me now what happens in each one of the places you go to, because I will tell you all the stories of my village and we'll see who wins."

Trafalgar smiled: "You want to know about Constancia."

"Well of course, she puzzles me; what do you think, you're the only curious person to set foot in the Burgundy?"

"Constancia had been lady-in-waiting to the queen, and each lady-in-waiting had the name of a virtue. Lady-in-waiting is a euphemism. They raised them strictly for that from the time they were little and afterwards the queen treated them like slaves, she kept them always shut up in miserable cells, one by one, which they left only to work like donkeys at the hardest, dirtiest, most humiliating tasks, and they starved them and punished them sometimes to the point of killing them. Constancia had gained the complicity of an idiot like Side who had fallen in love with her and, for years, with infinite patience, she stole things and gave them to her sweetheart and studied how to escape. And she escaped. And the guy, who worked in the port, had a ship ready for her loaded with everything, and she took off and headed in any old direction and landed on Donteä-Doreä. A slave who escapes isn't so important that they're going to chase her from world to world, but she had been through everything bearable and unbearable to make herself useful and agreeable and trustworthy and thus have a certain freedom of movement. And that was how she had learned secrets, secrets of the bedroom and of the throne room and of the bathroom and of behind the throne, and that made her dangerous. She knew they were going to find her, they were going to take her back and they were going to kill her slowly."

"Poor girl, it's not right."

"I didn't believe a word," said Trafalgar.

"But *che*, you don't like anyone."

"That woman had never been a slave in her life, I would have bet anything. She wasn't a beaten dog. She was Nefertiti, don't forget."

"And then?"

"Then the two of us acted moved and touched, and Side offered to take her to Sebdoepp, where she would be able to start a new life—the whole song—and she thanked him and I think she was sincere, something that also caught my attention. Why the hell didn't she tell the truth if she was truly afraid and was truly escaping from something?"

"Did you find out finally if she was escaping and what she was escaping from?"

"I think so. Of course, she could have lied again, but if she did lie again, I don't like the other solution I have to offer you one bit. Look, we spent the night there and she slept like an angel and Side and I took turns standing guard at my suggestion, just in case. I was annoyed but he had all he could want. The night was calm and in the morning we had breakfast with coffee and toast with butter and honey, and fruit juices and cake. When we finished, I asked Side to go downstairs to see if everything was still deserted and if we could leave, taking her along, and as the poor guy hadn't come down from the clouds, he went. I maneuvered to get myself behind her back, quite close, and suddenly I called her with an authoritative voice and when she turned around, I made as if to strike her. A slave would have shrunk to receive the blow. She drew herself up like a wild beast and if looks could kill, I wouldn't be telling this story, not even my ashes would have remained."

"So you were right."

"I don't know. I think so, I hope so. I told her, you were never a slave of anyone, Constancia, tell me if I'm mistaken but I think you were the one who had slaves at your service. When Side came back he found her crying and then he almost killed me. But as she cried like a queen and not like just anyone, she calmed down right away and told us the truth. Her Adrojanmarain existed as much as my Sondarbedo IV. She had been queen on Marrennen, there at the outer limits, a lost world, the last of a system of eleven around a burning sun where there were three races. The gods, who are invisible; the valid ones, who are people like you and me and like her and Side and everybody else; and the sleepers, who are these bestial idiots, like animals, who go around naked, bellowing all over the place without harming anyone, and who are fed and protected by order of the gods. All of this governed by a queen who is also a priestess. The office of queen isn't hereditary: those who hear the gods speak become queen. Only one in every generation. And each queen carries the name of a virtue. Constancia ascended the throne on the death of Clemencia, and from the time she was small, she knew she would be queen because she heard the voices of the invisible ones. And from up there on the throne she governed quite well, cared for and obeyed by her subjects, the valid ones who are the ones who do everything because the sleepers aren't good for anything and nobody sees the gods. But, here comes the but, you know there's always a but, once a year the priestess queen who hears voices has to personally meet with the invisible ones: she drinks a potion that puts her in a trance, they carry her to a temple carved into a mountain where no one enters but she, that single time each year, and there the gods appear to her."

"And then she sees them?"

"She sees them. Obviously the brunette had that square chin and that air of *I'm in charge here* for a reason. The first year she pretended to drink the syrup but she didn't drink any and she threw it away; she pretended to be asleep but she didn't sleep at all, they carried her to the temple and she didn't see anything nor did anyone appear to her. The second year, same story. The third year, she drank a few swallows and threw away the rest, she dozed a little and she woke up in the temple when she heard noises and whispers of people moving around her. And there, barely opening her eyes, she saw them."

"The gods?"

"Yes, the gods, the drooling brutes, the sleepers."

Jorge sat there with his mouth open and let his pipe go out and didn't even protest when Trafalgar calmly started on another cup of coffee.

"First she felt panic, she told us," Trafalgar said. "And then, like the good queen she was, and not only because she heard voices, she was absolutely enraged, she opened her eyes, stood up, and started yelling. And the beastly gods decided to beat it and she was left alone in the temple and she started to discover things. She found some doors, more or less hidden, through which the sleepers arrived from the other side of the mountain. And she deduced the rest. The brutes are in fact a kind of minor god, for household use only: beasts who only want to lie with the sun on their bellies and be fed and not be made to work and then have a big party with the reigning queen once a year. There's only one god-like thing about them and it's quite imperfect: a mild capacity for telepathic transmission—transmission, not reception. And in addition to the annual orgy, they use the priestess queen—who is elected, don't forget, because she has something of telepathic reception—to give orders: that they be fed, that they be protected, that temples be built, that this and that and the other be done."

"What garbage, old man."

"Garbage is putting it mildly. The girl left the temple the next day very coolly, she got together a few technicians and told them the gods had ordered an expedition to who knows where and that in less than a day a ship had to be ready, equipped for a single crewmember, with furniture, food, books, pictures—anyway, everything we saw there. And that night she had the port cleared, she climbed into the ship alone and she took off and went as far away as possible and got as far as she could and almost killed herself landing on Donteä-Doreä which, unfortunately for her, had been deserted for centuries."

"And had she been there a long time?"

"Fairly long. More than a Marrennen year, that's why she was afraid. She had left the brutes deprived three years running and then she had escaped. And her successor must have gone into the temple at least once by now, and the brutish gods combine pleasure and practicality, so they must have given the order to look for her."

"You got her out of there, I imagine."

"Now I see that, yes, you're a romantic, too, like Side, and not only because you've written the *Manifesto of a Romantic.* But don't you see that woman is a walking danger? And that if she once defied and defeated the brutes, gods or sleepers or demons or whatever they are, she's quite capable of defying and defeating them as often as she cares to? For myself, I'd have left her on Donteä-Doreä so she could work out the dispute once and for all when the Marrennen folk arrived. Relax, Side is a mechanic, not a poet, but he succeeded in having us take her along. Which is to say, he took her, because as for me, even if she were the very, very best of her kind, I wouldn't touch her with tongs."

"I can already see you being chased back and forth by the naked brutes."

"The naked brutes don't trouble me a bit, one by one or all together. She is the one to be feared. I saw her. I looked her in the eyes when I made is if to hit her and she confronted me. Look, Jorge, ever since I returned from Sebdoepp, where I unloaded the two of them, ever since then I've been asking myself who the invisible gods of Marrennen are. Listen, Marcos, how much is it? Don't do that to me, I'm the one who invited you. Yes, because either the other queens who were named Piedad or Templanza or Caridad were nitwits and never brought themselves to talk about what they undoubtedly must have realized happened to them when they were asleep in the temple, or there is on Marrennen, poor Side, a race of gods who are not the brutes, they're the queens. And they are the ones who hold the annual orgy, not the poor unfortunates. Belonging to that race would explain her lies. Although yes, I already know what you're going to say, those lies can be explained with a dozen innocent reasons. But if the invisible gods are the queens, then Constancia escaped because she betrayed them, I don't care how but certainly for a single motive: in search of more power."

"I think you're probably right."

"Let's be going," said Trafalgar.

"I'd almost have preferred to have gone to the office and done all the things I'm behind on," said Jorge as they left. "If you see a brunette, warn me so I can look the other way."

Strelitzias, Lagerstroemias, and Gypsophila

It had been so long since I'd seen him! Me busy with my books, he travelling, we had talked on the phone a few times and had promised to see each other and it seemed the moment never came. And one fine day, with no previous phone call, we ran into each other on the pedestrian mall, big hug and how are you and you look very well and, very formal and proper, we went into the Burgundy to have a coffee. Marcos served us personally because, he says, none of those clumsy waiters when Trafalgar comes in, although his waiters are never clumsy.

"Two coffees," Trafalgar said after the greetings.

"And a big glass of soda water," I said.

Just a few minutes and we had the coffees in front of us. I looked at him a little surprised.

"What is it?" he asked.

"Ummm . . . ," I said, with a *now what do I say* face.

"Yes," he said, "I gave up smoking. So what?"

"You-gave-up-smo-king," I enunciated.

"Yes. Eritrea doesn't like me to smoke."

"Eritrea? What do you have, a cat or a dog or a canary allergic to smoke?"

"My daughter. Eritrea is my daughter."

I think I fainted. Maybe not, but nearly: the world started spinning around like a top, of course the world is always spinning, but not so fast, and the most I could do was hold on tight to my chair and close my eyes.

When I managed to open them, Trafalgar was fanning me with the Burgundy's coffee menu and Marcos was patting my hand and telling me I was going to be just fine.

Then Trafalgar began to tell me, little by little and detailing every encounter, because the thing had already been going on for years, but I swear it is all true.

THE FIRST TIME

"I can't be responsible for her," said Guinevera Lapis Lazuli or whatever her name was.

"She" was a little girl not this high off the ground who played at jumping, talking to herself, and throwing a colored ball up in the air.

"She's yours," said Guinevera, "so your alternatives are to take her with you or put her in an orphanage."

Trafalgar almost had an attack, one because he remembered his adventure with Lapis Lazuli and two because the girl was undoubtedly his, black eyes and impertinent jaw and a way of lifting her head; and then also because thinking of letting her go to an orphanage made him feel like a heartless swine. And Trafalgar is many things, but a heartless swine he is not.

He called her: "We're going on a trip," he said. "Do you know who I am?"

"My papa," she said and won him over forever.

Two words, only two words and she had achieved what no one else had, so far as I know—and, for the record, I know plenty about Trafalgar. The number of women who had tried not only to win him but to keep him by force of sweet nothings and those Barbie and Doris Day or whatever type things, and not one ever got anywhere save that little pipsqueak who said "my papa" and okay, all set. Cursed be those loudmouthed machistas who make themselves out to be supermen and a baby won't make them cry because men don't cry but they do turn to butter.

"What's her name?" he asked Guinevera because he couldn't meet the child's (black) eyes.

"Eristemiádica Perlingheredisti."

Which sounds more like Greek but is Veroboariano.

"You're crazy," Trafalgar said and he left with the girl and this is something: he brought her to Rosario.

On the trip he told her: "Your name is Eritrea from now on, okay? Eritrea Perla Medrano."

She agreed and repeated it softly as if it were a Jabberwocky, Eritrea Perla Medrano, eritreaperla Medrano, eritreaperlamedrano, et cetera. And the thing is, he liked those names: they resembled the nonsense Lapis Lazuli had given him and they were, like his own, the names of battles, two instead of only one: the Italians marching to conquest and Pearl Harbor attacked by the Axis.

CHILDHOOD

They arrived home late but Crisóstoma was waiting for them with supper ready. That is, she was waiting for him and he showed up with the girl.

"She's hungry," Trafalgar said without offering further explanations.

Crisóstoma has the soul of a hen, she spread her wing and took her under it, soft and cozy. "But of course!" she scolded Trafalgar. "I'm sure you gave her nothing to eat, poor thing. What's your name?"

She didn't know who the girl was or why she was there but she wasn't going to let her go hungry for anything in the world.

"Eritrea Perla Medrano."

And then Rogelio arrived, in robe and pajamas, thanks to which Crisóstoma didn't faint like me in the Burgundy, and the pipsqueak had both of them in her pocket within a minute and a quarter. They gave her thin oatmeal, a chicken drumstick, sweet potato conserve, and Coca-Cola. Not because Trafalgar drinks Coca-Cola, *vade retro*, but because Rogelio does and he always has a bottle in the refrigerator.

That same night, while Eritrea sucked on a candy (Rogelio once again—a bon vivant), between the three of them they removed the stereo and the old armchair and the floor lamp from the room next to Trafalgar's bedroom and they made up the bed and put feather pillows on it, a little bedside table with a lamp with an alabaster shade that had been in the living room, and a little bell so she could call if she wanted something, anything at all, water or more Coca-Cola or company or for someone to tell her a story or whatever occurred to her.

The next day they went to the civil registry with Rogelio and Crisóstoma as witnesses.

"I've come to register the girl," said Trafalgar.

"What?" said a fat lady with badly dyed ash-blonde hair and a doughy, underbaked face. "At that age and not registered yet?"

"No."

After snorts and protests, the fat lady asked, "Name?"

"Eritrea Perla Medrano."

"Daughter of?"

"Trafalgar Medrano, here's my identity card."

"Birth certificate?"

"I don't have it. It was lost in the fire."

The fat lady started to perspire.

"Name of the mother."

"Mother unknown," said Trafalgar.

"What do you mean, unknown?" exploded the fat lady.

"Well, see," Trafalgar said and proceeded to tell the fat lady a whole novel about a frenzied orgy in which everyone with everyone—you follow me, right? And in which, well, when he got to the juicy details the fat lady, pale and sweaty, said good, that's fine, unknown, yes, certainly, fire, what a shame, well, yes.

At school, things went splendidly well. Little starched apron, little braids, black shoes with white ankle socks, clean hands, freshly brushed teeth, and twenty cents for a cocoa and five little cookies during the long recess, adorable.

After about two months, they called him: "Señor Medrano, you must know that girls enter this institution before learning to read or, moreover, doing sums. Eritrea gets bored and of course, as she was previously taught that which it is the task of the school . . ."

"I beg your pardon," said Trafalgar, "but no one taught her anything. She learns on her own, just from watching. She's a very intelligent girl," and he restrained himself from adding, "like her father."

"There is no doubt of that," said the vice principal, her lips tight. It seemed she did not like the girls of her school to be intelligent.

"We will attempt, of course, to discipline her a little, because as she is quick to learn, she spends her time, I don't know, for example in haranguing her classmates to, in a manner of speaking, avoid calligraphy class or scare Señora de Romero, who teaches mathematics."

"Look, better you not discipline her too much. I am of the opinion that children should be allowed to express themselves freely, ma'am."

"Miss."

"Miss. Discipline is very fine for barracks, but in school one has to be seeing what each student's like and what she wants. Talk to the girls, see, and find out why they do what they do."

"Very modern," said the vice principal, almost without separating her lips, which was quite the achievement.

But, obviously, by fourth grade he could clearly see that it was impossible to keep Eritrea in school. Not only did she do all that the vice principal had told him, but she sweet-talked or led her classmates in trying to get the punishment reduced for a girl who had been rebellious or to protest because they didn't let them play soccer (that's not for girls!) or to go to school in costume (pirates, ghosts, Russian princesses and odalisques were the favorites).

Trafalgar took her home, improvised a study room beside the library, brought in Juan Grela, who lived quite close by, once a week to teach her painting, and sent her to the Cosettinis' school and everyone was happy.

ADOLESCENCE

I met her when she was already an adolescent, because all of the foregoing happened almost in secret (Trafalgar was embarrassed to have a daughter) and punctuated by his trips as he came and went, leaving the girl with Crisóstoma, who seemed like the grandmother and Rogelio, who was grandfather, chauffer, advisor, butler, and errand boy all at the same time.

She was a beauty. She's still a beauty but now she's a woman, sensational. Sometimes I think the vice principal was right.

At that moment, after the surprise, the fainting and so forth, she was tall and thin, with two enormous eyes like coals they were so, so black. Hair almost chestnut (like her mother, Trafalgar told me much later, on a day of modest confidences), a powerful nose, both straight and fine, large mouth, and a neck that allowed her to raise her head like a swan. Gorgeous. Trafalgar was crazy about her and just like Jorge, said he had already bought the shotgun and had it under the table ready to fill the first mother's son ¡#%!!+°=¡!#~* *grrr* who might get close to his girl full of lead. She laughed.

"You won't even find out," she said.

"It's a joke," he told me, but he was plenty uneasy.

She passed, Eritrea Perla, all her exams with perfect scores all the way through high school and then Trafalgar asked her what she wanted to study.

"I want to be a gardener," she said.

"Kindergarten teacher?"

"No! Gardener, gar-den-er, take care of gardens, cure trees that are sick, plant flowers, prune, cut the grass, grafting and layering, all that. Besides, I always liked playing with mud."

"Where did you get that silly idea?" asked the indignant father.

"I read it in *Kalpa Imperial*, what of it? It says gardeners are wise people because they see the world from where one ought to, from below, in contact with the earth. And that they are always good humored. And the garden at this house is a mess and Atilio doesn't even know how to water much less put each plant where it goes and I want strelitzias, lagerstroemias, and gypsophila."

There was a kind of family conflict, a generation gap and all the rest; arguments and tantrums, no, because Eritrea was never one for tantrums, but bribes and blackmail, yes. And, of course, the girl became a gardener. At the beginning, a little on her own, and later more seriously, taking the courses from the municipality with a doctorate offered at Juan's place three times a week from nine to twelve. She worked in their own garden and in all the gardens in the neighborhood. Winter was especially cold that year.

"Take me with you," she said to him one horribly windy, cold day after having covered all the plants to protect them from frost.

"Not even if I were crazy," said Trafalgar.

He took her.

They went to Susakiiri-Do with a cargo of reels and reams and tons of paper of every kind, thickness, and color. Susakiiri-Do was a land of earthquakes and a few years back had had one of the strongest, so strong it almost finished off the world, and the aftermath had unleashed plagues and fires. The population had been recovering, but there were no libraries or bookstores left and there was nowhere to get wood to make paper, let alone rags. Memory had been preserved, because like a good, civilized people, that of Susakiiri-Do included some who knew the old books (and the new ones, too) word by word and sum by sum. But they had to be written down and for that reason Trafalgar went there punctually every six months taking the paper on which they could be reproduced.

There the Maestre General, who was sort of like a president of the whole world, awaited them: Susakiiri-Do is a small and peaceful world. With one president, who is elected every I don't remember how many years but it's not very many, and a kind of Council of Elders and Notables, that's enough. They housed Trafalgar and Eritrea in the presidential palace. He stayed at the clunker to supervise the unloading and she went sightseeing. They took her to see the parks, the narrow, peaceful river that crossed the city, the monuments to something or someone, the elegant streets, and the library-in-progress, which was in an enormous building but still had very few books, magazines, pamphlets, all those things a library has.

In the evening, she was invited to dine with the Maestre and his wife. They ate agariostes with czor sauce (agariostes are a kind of rabbit smaller than ours and that like ours are a plague and so no one feels bad about eating them and they have a white, spicy, tender meat;

the czor is like a carrot but green and much softer and with a flavor almost, almost like a leek) and for dessert cream of curí with zyminia seeds and they drank a rather sweet white wine that Eritrea didn't like at all but she faked it as much as she could, which, it has to be said, is never much.

In the middle of dessert, Eritrea jumped up and said, "Where is my father?"

"There, there honey, he'll come," said the Maestre's wife. "He must have been delayed with the unloading."

"He should have been here by now," said Eritrea, and she ran out.

The Maestre and his wife sat there astonished, their spoons in the air as if frozen and unable to go on eating.

Without looking back and without caring a bit either what her hosts were doing or what they would think of her, Eritrea ran, ran, ran. She heard voices that she left behind her but she didn't stop running.

"Miss, listen miss!" someone shouted while she was running.

But that someone was in a vehicle and caught up with her almost immediately.

"Where are you going? It's nighttime. This road doesn't lead anywhere."

It was a great big man dressed in orange and green (on Susakiiri-Do everyone wears loud colors) and with a scarlet cap with black pompoms. Even as she kept running, she managed to see it was all very respectable.

"Ah," the man with the pompoms recognized her, "you're the daughter of the merchant who sells us the paper. Come, climb in and I'll take you."

"Not back, not back!" she said.

"No, no, of course not! I'll take you wherever you want to go. Come on, climb in."

Eritrea said to herself, in the midst of her desperate hurry, that the best thing to do would be to climb into the vehicle that was a kind of huge, square car and that way they would arrive faster although she wasn't very sure where or in what direction that place might be.

"This way, this way, I'm almost sure it's this way," she said, "that we left the clunker for the unloading."

"I know, I know, everyone's talking about that, it's a big event when the paper arrives. I know where it is."

Quickly, quickly and silently, they went toward the place. The owner of the vehicle was worried about the road, which wasn't exactly a smooth, straight route with no obstacles but rather just the contrary. Large rocks impeded their passage and smaller, rough stones jumped when the wheels bit them. She didn't know what it was. Maybe ruins from the last earthquake, or an abandoned road as the man with the car said. But they had to continue that way, she was sure of that.

"You can see something over there," the man said. "A light."

It wasn't a light, it was only a reflection, barely the faint glow of something that rose up from the ground. Eritrea told him to hurry.

"I'm doing what I can, miss," said the man, who jumped in his seat and set the pompoms swaying over his forehead every time they went over a rock that was larger than the others.

The light was like a wound. It looked like a wound, a brilliant gash. A wound in the earth. But all that mattered to Eritrea was that Trafalgar was lying—unconscious, it appeared—with his eyes closed, his hands slack, one foot touching the wound of light in the ground.

"Help me," she said to the man.

They jumped down and between them, dragging him, lifting him as much as they could, they carried him to the vehicle. Getting him inside it was another thing again. It was impossible even between the two of them to lift the weight of the weak body that they couldn't manipulate. What they did was sit him down on the ground with his back supported by the mudguards that almost completely covered the wheel. Better backrest, impossible. When Eritrea saw that Trafalgar was breathing well and trying to open his eyes and move his hands, she left him to the care of the man and ran toward the light. The man with the car yelled at her to come back but she didn't pay any attention.

Without running now, deliberately, carefully, she approached the light in the ground and leaned over. Leaned over is saying a lot: she tried to lean over but she wasn't able to because it flashed so brightly that it hurt her eyes. She moved her head back and then little by little, with her eyes closed and barely separating the lids, she tried to look. It was like looking at the sun. She closed her eyes again and retreated again and did that several times until she was able to see something. The sun under the ground: she wanted to laugh but the urge went away immediately because there was something there in the deep sun. Shadows, it seemed to her, they were moving in the light down below. Far below.

"It can't be," she said.

She picked up a stone from the ground and let it fall into the crack of light. There was a confusion below, like something boiling in which dark waves moved; no, not dark because it wasn't possible that there be dark in that light. Waves that shone less than that which surrounded them.

The man yelled at her to come back. Trafalgar opened his eyes and said, "Eritrea?"

"Let's go back," she said.

She sat beside Trafalgar and the vehicle backed up (it seems like a jeep, Trafalgar said), turned around, and returned to the road.

"It's over," she said.

"What is?" Trafalgar wanted to know.

"What made you fall in the light. It's passed but we have to tell them."

"Eri, I don't understand anything," said Trafalgar, his voice hoarse, the words unsteady.

"Don't worry. I do understand."

Trafalgar turned stony. Lousy snot-nose, he thought, who does she think she is? I'm the one who's used to explaining, practically no one ever understands anything and then I go and I explain and now along comes this kid who's not even twenty years old and it turns out she's the one who explains, come on. She was right, of course, but he consoled himself thinking that with the fainting (what was it that had made him lose consciousness? He remembered nothing, except feeling heat, a heat that rose up from his ankles to his neck, an unbearable heat) he was still a little dazed and couldn't think straight.

In the palace, the Maestre and his wife and a few officials were waiting for them. Everyone had a worried face and everyone sighed with relief when they saw them arrive.

"My friend, my friend," said the Maestre and he took Trafalgar's hand between his own and shook it up and down and down and up.

"How are you, you sweet thing, how are you?" asked the Maestre's wife, unable to bring herself to take Eritrea by the hand or embrace her or anything like that.

The man with the jeep and the pompoms got out with them and stayed there, close by, and as no one paid any attention to him, either to kick him out or to shake his hand, he decided not to move until he found out what was happening and why that girl was doing what she was doing.

Eritrea asked the Maestre General to gather the Council and all those who had any authority on that world. Trafalgar, sitting very tense, very serious in an armchair, witnessed the whole spectacle. The Maestre wasn't going to pay attention just like that to a girl who asked him for such a thing, but Trafalgar was a respected person in Susakiiri-Do and people believed what he said.

"Fine," said the Maestre, "they're on their way."

"The earthquakes," said Trafalgar, "aren't just movements of the earth. There's something down there below."

"But that's just a tall tale," protested one of the elders, "a legend for gullible old women."

"Oh, really?" said Eritrea. "They're not legends. I saw them."

And she told what she had seen.

"The firewellers exist? That's impossible!"

"I don't know what they're called, but they exist," she said.

"So, sir," said Trafalgar, "tell us."

"They say, ahem, ahem, uhh, well, that there are some beings, some animals—they're not people, right?—they don't speak nor do they dress or have tools or bury their dead, they're animals that lived on Susakiiri-Do before we arrived and when we arrived and they realized they couldn't get rid of us, they took refuge underground. They eat fire, that's what they say, not that I believe it, they eat fire and they produce fire. And when the fire floods the subterranean caves, it starts to come out and that causes the earthquakes. Tall tales, like the good Maestre said."

"Well, no," said Trafalgar.

THE END (FOR NOW)

Eritrea told what she had seen:

"At first I thought it was hell," she said, "but no horned devil with tail and trident came out of there, so it wasn't that. The heat was like hell, that's true. No, of course, I was never in hell but it was a cold heat, like swords. I know what I'm saying isn't very coherent, but try to imagine it: an atrocious heat but not from fire, on that I agree with all of you, they eat fire and produce fire. No: it's heat and the fire of red-hot iron at the moment it becomes steel. And it gets into your bones, like cold."

Trafalgar was delighted, because that was exactly what he, even without leaning over as Eritrea had done, just getting very close, had felt before he lost all notion of time and space and had fallen backwards—luckily, not forward.

The Maestre General and his wife and the big men of the Council listened rapt but both Trafalgar and Eritrea saw they didn't believe them. She, who hasn't lived as much as Trafalgar and hasn't yet learned to keep quiet when it is necessary to say nothing (she will probably never learn) began shouting: "But why don't you believe us? Are you idiots or what? Aren't you going to do anything?"

"Do?" said the Maestre. "But no, child, there is no need to do anything."

Eritrea hates being called *child* or *honey* or, even worse, *sweetie.*

Before she could bellow that she had a name and was nobody's sweetie or child, Trafalgar stood up, he grabbed her by the arm and told her all right, all right, our delightful hosts are right, they know more than we, there's no need to get like that.

The girl has learned something along the way. She looked into his (black) eyes and said fine, of course, she had had a shock, she wanted to go to bed.

It was a quiet night. Eritrea lay down and pretended to sleep. And when she heard Trafalgar go into the bedroom they had assigned him next to hers, she sat up in bed and waited. Not long. She was becoming impatient but the door opened softly and closed softly and Trafalgar came in and sat on the bed.

"Well," he said, also softly.

"These aren't decent people," said Eritrea.

"Wait a minute, wait a minute."

"No, seriously, they're not decent."

"Go on, why?"

"They know what's down there."

"Because they are what's down there," Trafalgar finished.

"You knew?"

"I suspected it just as you suspected something was happening to me. They wanted to make us believe that it's all a lie but you and I know it's true."

"And the guy in the jeep who took me didn't want to let me get close once we'd gotten you away from the edge of the crack. Also, what's that about they came from somewhere? Weren't they from here? Why? Do they go from world to world eating fire and destroying the place they've come to? And the worst of it is the matter of the library."

"What's the matter with the library?"

"You haven't seen it but I have. The building is gigantic but inside there aren't more than six or seven bookcases with a few books. Don't you come every six months bringing paper so they can copy the books that according to them were lost in the earthquake? Well, where is all that paper if they haven't written more than fifty or sixty books, huh?"

"They ate it," said Trafalgar.

"Exactly. They feed the bonfire with paper. There are no trees here and even you can't bring them. You could probably bring a few itty-bitty ones but they can't wait for them to grow."

They were silent for a while.

"What do they do?" she said. "Do they change form to go down to the depths of the world to feed themselves with fire?"

"Could be."

And they were quiet again.

"We're in danger," said Trafalgar.

"Let's leave now," said Eritrea almost at the same time.

But after thinking it over, they decided to stay and see what happened. Because if they tried to escape that night, someone would surely stop them. They knew, the firewellers, that they knew. Or that they suspected. And for that reason they would have them under surveillance. In sum: that night, impossible. All the same, they worked out an escape plan for the next day, just in case, in which the main point was that they should not separate or be separated.

And the next day the Maestre General and his wife and everyone and possibly the pompom man as well, although they didn't see him around, were more agreeable and obliging than ever. After breakfast they invited Trafalgar to an office where, they said, they were going to pay him. Trafalgar put on an astonished face.

"But I still have part of the cargo in the clunker," he said, "the most interesting part. It's an experimental paper, heavy and very smooth, that comes already cut into pages. It has its drawbacks, however. I could only get them to give me a small quantity because it's still under study. It seems it burns too easily."

As bait, it was so coarse as to be unbelievable, but Eritrea had approved the attempt: "If they are what we think they are," she had said, "they're going to swallow it hook, line, and sinker."

They swallowed it.

"Come help me," Trafalgar said to Eritrea.

And off the two of them went, feeling that their backs prickled and the hair on the nape of their necks stood up stiff like a cat's when it gets angry, almost sure they were going to pounce on them any minute and drag them to the depths of the small, happy, peaceful, cultured world of Susakiiri-Do where they were going to burn as if in hell, or worse, where they were going to become firewellers and they, too, were going to feed on fire and they were going to live forever in the underground of a world of earthquakes and monsters.

I am happy to be able to say that nothing happened. Gazed upon by the placid and smiling faces of Susakiiri-Do's notables, they got into the clunker, closed the hatches, started it up, and they left. The Maestre General and his people watched them while they lifted off and kept watching them long after, so long they almost broke their necks trying to see how the clunker became a little black dot in the blue sky.

Eritrea, who kept her eye on them, said: "Might we have been mistaken?"

"Don't talk nonsense," said Trafalgar.

THE END, END

"You won't have taken her along again on any other trips," I said.

"Why not?" he said. "Sometimes when I know nothing is going to happen to us, she comes with me. So long, of course, as it's not the season for planting or pruning or germinating or what do I know, or for taking care of the strelitzias. She has a bunch of clients in the neighborhood."

I told him I was happy, although I like lagerstroemias better, especially the purple ones, and gypsophila is always nice to make a bouquet shine. And as far as knowing what's going to happen, I told him no one ever knows what's going to happen to them or what isn't going to happen. That, for example, Eritrea is going to introduce a boyfriend one of these days. . . and I stopped talking because I saw his face.

"Don't tell me," I reacted. "What's the guy like?"

"An idiot," he said. "A useless fool who doesn't smoke or drink wine or know how to prepare a barbecue, who works out and studies dentistry and doesn't play chess. The worst."

"Trafalgar, you don't play chess."

"Fine, but the guy is an idiot. And to top it off, he's a Ñuls man. Can you imagine me with a leper son-in-law? And if she comes and tells me she's going to marry same, I'll kick her out of the house."

I laughed for a good long time.

"She's going to have several—many, I hope—before marrying the one she chooses. Don't worry. Perhaps he'll be a riffraff die-hard and not a leper."[2]

"I hope so."

"And may she give you a bunch of grandchildren."

"Grandchildren? Me, grandchildren?"

"I hope they're granddaughters," I said.

What he answered is irreproducible, but what do I care?

---

2 The riffraff are Rosario Central. Leprosy is Ñuls. Riffraff and lepers are, of course, irreconcilable. (Author's note.)

Trafalgar and I

"Because there are things that can't be told," said Trafalgar on that stormy day. "How do you say them? What name do you give them? What verbs do you use? Is there a suitable language for that? Not richer, not more flowery, but that takes into account other things? I was on a world without a name, covered with forests and swamps, full of monstrous animals that didn't take any notice of me, and in a clearing in the forest, in a white wooden house with metal screens in the windows and a weathervane on the ridge, there was a man sitting at a table in the gallery drinking tea. I sat down with him and he served tea for me. Afterwards I came home. That's all."

It started to rain. A beetle crawled under a magnolia leaf and a cold drop hit me on the forehead.

About the Author

Angélica Gorodischer, daughter of the writer Angélica de Arcal, was born in 1929 in Buenos Aires and has lived most of her life in Rosario, Argentina. From her first book of stories, she has displayed a mastery of science-fiction themes, handled with her own personal slant, and exemplary of the South American fantasy tradition. Her more than twenty books include *Kalpa Imperial, Prodigios,* and *Tumba de jaguares.* She has received many awards for her work, including most recently the World Fantasy Lifetime Achievement Award.

About the Translator

Amalia Gladhart (amaliagladhart.com) is the translator of two novels by Ecuadorian novelist Alicia Yánez Cossío, *The Potbellied Virgin* (2006) and *Beyond the Islands* (2011). Her chapbook *Detours* won the 2011 Burnside Review Fiction Chapbook Contest. Her poetry and short fiction have appeared in *Iowa Review, Bellingham Review, Stone Canoe,* and elsewhere. She is Professor of Spanish at the University of Oregon.

Recent and forthcoming short story collections and novels from
Small Beer Press for independently minded readers:

Georges-Olivier Châteaureynaud, *A Life on Paper: Stories*
"The celebrated Châteaureynaud."—*New York Times*

Ted Chiang, *Stories of Your Life and Others*
"Shining, haunting, mind-blowing tales"—Junot Díaz (*The Brief Wondrous Life of Oscar Wao*)

Karen Joy Fowler, *What I Didn't See and Other Stories*
"An exceptionally versatile author."—*St. Louis Post-Dispatch*

Angélica Gorodischer, *Kalpa Imperial* (trans. Ursula K. Le Guin)
"Speaks of self-evident wisdom while itself remaining mysterious."—*Washington Post*

Elizabeth Hand, *Errantry: Stories*
"Elegant nightmares, sensuously told."—*Publishers Weekly*

Kij Johnson, *At the Mouth of the River of Bees: Stories*
"Thought-provoking . . . emotionally wrenching stories."—*Publishers Weekly,* Best Books of the Year

The Unreal and the Real: Selected Stories of Ursula K. Le Guin
In two volumes: *Where on Earth* & *Outer Space, Inner Land*
"No better spirit in all of American letters than that of Ursula K. Le Guin."—*Slate*

Kelly Link, *Magic for Beginners; Stranger Things Happen*

Karen Lord, *Redemption in Indigo*
Mythopoeic, Crawford, & Frank Collymore Award winner

Maureen F. McHugh, *After the Apocalypse: Stories*
"Incisive, contemporary, and always surprising."—*Publishers Weekly* Top 10 Books of the Year

Geoff Ryman, *Paradise Tales*
"Includes one of the most powerful stories I've read in the last 10 years."—*New York Times*

Sofia Samatar, *A Stranger in Olondria**
"Samatar's sensual descriptions create a rich, strange landscape, allowing a lavish adventure to
unfold that is haunting and unforgettable."—*Library Journal* (starred review)

**Forthcoming*
Our ebooks are available from our indie press ebooksite:

www.weightlessbooks.com

www.smallbeerpress.com

31901051788067